THE MEANING IN MISTLETOE

a Poppy Creek novel

RACHAEL BLOOME

Cover design: Ana Grigoriu-Voicu with Books-design

Editing: Beth Attwood

Proofing: Krista Dapkey with KD Proofreading

SERIES READING ORDER

THE CLAUSE IN CHRISTMAS

THE TRUTH IN TIRAMISU

THE SECRET IN SANDCASTLES

THE MEANING IN MISTLETOE

THE FAITH IN FLOWERS

Mom,
*For being my mother, mentor, and best friend. And for inspiring me
with your loving, generous heart.*

LETTER FROM THE AUTHOR

*D*ear Friends,
       Each book in the Poppy Creek series is inspired by one of my favorite passages in the Bible: 1 Corinthians 13: 4-8, which describes the attributes of love.

This book, in particular, focuses on love's generous spirit.

Of course, generosity can manifest in many forms, as we will explore in Jack and Kat's story, but one facet is with our physical possessions. There's tremendous joy in sharing what we have with those around us—near and far—especially during the holidays.

As I prayed about practical ways to better embody this mindset in my own life, God drew my attention to this book itself. And I began to wonder what it would look like to give a portion of the proceeds to a charitable foundation in perpetuity. While I was prayerfully considering this idea, my sister began volunteering at an organization called The Refuge, which provides housing and much-needed resources to women rescued from human trafficking. Needless to say, the idea quickly became a reality.

Thus, with each book sold, you and I are partnering together to support this wonderful ministry. If you're curious about the work they're doing, you can learn more at rfwlasvegas.org.

Is there a cause or charity you're passionate about? I'd love to hear about it! You can reach me at hello@rachaelbloome.com or in my Facebook reader group, Rachael Bloome's Secret Garden Club.

Meanwhile, I hope you enjoy returning to Poppy Creek and visiting with old friends.

Blessings & Blooms,

CHAPTER 1

*B*linking against unwanted tears, Kat Bennet let the soft cotton cloth fall away, revealing a porcelain nativity set. At the sight of the familiar scene, the emotions she'd fought all evening escaped in a strangled sob.

Fern Flores set a plush snowman on the coffee table before reaching over to pat Kat's hand. "What's wrong, *mija?*" The older woman's motherly endearment only added to Kat's melancholy. Oh, how she would miss her.

"It's nothing." Kat roughly wiped her damp cheeks with her knuckles, annoyed she'd succumbed to her sadness even after promising herself she'd keep it together.

"Nothing?" Fern's dark eyes narrowed into skeptical slits, accentuating the deep grooves around the edges—her "laugh lines," as she affectionately called them.

As a self-proclaimed realist, Kat marveled at Fern's ability to look on the bright side. The kindhearted caretaker could put a positive spin on almost anything—including wrinkles. But Kat knew the telltale creases could come from other avenues besides laughter. In fact, most of the lines that had been etched into her late mother's hardened features could be traced to the bottom of a bottle—either alcohol or prescription, sometimes worse.

Shoving the bitter memories to the back of her mind where they belonged, Kat focused her gaze on the amber flames flickering in the fireplace, willing the tears away. The rich, velvety timbre of Nat King Cole's "The Christmas Song" filled the silence as she collected her thoughts. "I can't believe this might be our last Christmas in this house."

"Don't lose hope. There's still time for a miracle."

"I suppose so." Despite her overwhelming doubts, Kat attempted a small smile as she resumed unpacking the Christmas decorations.

She'd try to be strong for Fern's sake, but it would take more than a miracle to save Hope Hideaway. After losing two of their top donors, the women's shelter had been bleeding money for months. They'd reached out for help—the small town of Starcross Cove took care of its own—but the entire community was struggling after a coastal storm left several businesses and homes damaged. Mayor Thompson promised to do what she could for the shelter, but her aid would sadly be too little too late. At this rate, Hope Hideaway would have to close by the end of the year.

And yet, Fern still refused to turn anyone away. The large historic beach house with a detached bungalow had maintained full occupancy in all six of its bedrooms, somehow managing to operate on a meager budget. Not that any of the women noticed the financial strain since Fern whipped up the most scrumptious, flavorful meals despite her scant ingredients.

The tantalizing aroma of cinnamon and sugar wafted from the kitchen, causing Kat's mouth to water. Every December 1, without fail, Fern baked several batches of her famous Christmas cookies—a top secret family recipe she affectionately called *Pequeños Milagros* or Tiny Miracles, Milagros for short. They were a huge hit among Hope Hideaway residents as well as the community center down the street.

Kat glanced at the clock above the ornate mantel. The women would be back home any minute from their computer science class. That was the other "nonnegotiable" draining their funds. One of the conditions for staying at Hope Hideaway included mandatory classes at the community center, paid for by the shelter. While Kat loved the idea on principle, and even taught a weekly self-defense class, she couldn't deny the effect on their dwindling bank account.

"Remember this?" Fern unwrapped a small gingerbread house made from polymer clay.

"Of course. How could I forget?" Kat traced the smooth rooftop with her fingertips. Colleen Hannigan's daughter, Daisy, had made it during their first Christmas at Hope Hideaway. For several weeks, the seven-year-old girl wouldn't speak or make eye contact with anyone. But when Fern brought out the molding clay one cozy, winter evening, the little girl came alive. The mother-daughter duo stayed for a total of three months, and by the time they'd left, Daisy had transformed into a vibrant, talkative butterfly.

From the first day Hope Hideaway opened its doors, Fern had maintained the same policy—the women could stay as long as they needed, but eventually, they'd have to move on, armed with the necessary skills for a fresh start. No one should hide forever, she always said.

When Fern started the shelter, she had one goal in mind—give the women hope, then help them settle into a home of their own. She even gave each resident a hope chest to begin the process of building a new and better life. And for nearly thirty years, that's exactly what she'd done... until now.

Come January 1, Hope Hideaway might cease to exist.

Unless Kat found a way to save it.

*R*aising one eyebrow, Jack Gardener folded his burly arms in front of his chest.

"C'mon, one taste." His persistent sous-chef flashed a challenging smirk. "What? Afraid you'll actually like it?"

Jack grunted. Hiring his childhood friend, Colt Davis, to work at his restaurant had simultaneously been the best and worst decision of the century. Although he'd been glad to provide a part-time job so Colt could stay in town, the incessant culinary experiments were driving him crazy. He liked owning a down-to-earth, no-frills barbecue joint with the best burgers and sarsaparilla floats in Poppy Creek. And he planned to keep it that way.

"I already put your strange cinnamon-and-coffee steaks on the menu, isn't that enough?"

"Are you referring to the steaks that won the Fourth of July cook-off?" Colt rebutted, his impish grin revealing the dimple in his left cheek.

"Steaks shouldn't be sweet," Jack mumbled. "Clearly, the judges had heatstroke."

Colt rolled his eyes, shoving the spoon toward him. "Just try it."

Squinting at the syrupy sauce, Jack wrinkled his nose. "What is it?"

"It's an espresso molasses glaze. It'll go great with the brisket."

The furrow in Jack's brow deepened. Why couldn't Colt leave well enough alone? The Buttercup Bistro across the street could cater to the tourists with their fancy-schmancy menu, while they focused on local favorites like grilled tri-tip and his twice-baked potatoes.

"Open wide," his friend said in a singsong voice, brandishing the serving utensil like an airplane. "You have a one-way ticket to I told you so."

"Give me that." After snatching the spoon, Jack slurped the

6

bizarre concoction. He tried to keep his expression stoic, but to his consternation, the glaze didn't taste half bad. *Drat.* He really didn't want to change the menu again. Especially since Colt seemed bent on turning his humble establishment—which started as a bare-bones diner—into a Michelin star restaurant. And the last thing Jack wanted was a deluge of snobby tourists who cared more about the price tag of the plate than the food itself.

"Ha! I knew you'd like it!" Colt pumped his fist in triumph. "Can I put it on the menu for this weekend?"

Setting the utensil back on the spoon rest, Jack untied his plaid waist apron. "We'll discuss it later. We don't want to be late for Luke's special get-together for Cassie."

"No kidding. He hasn't stopped talking about it all week." Colt shoved the lid on the saucepan. "The way he's been droning on and on about it, you'd think he was giving her the Hope Diamond instead of some old scrapbook."

"It's not any old scrapbook. The Christmas Calendar is what brought your brother and Cassie together. You really should sit down and hear the whole story sometime. As far as love stories go, it's pretty epic," Jack told him before swiveling to address his other cook. "Johnson, we should be back in twenty. Hold down the fort."

Vick Johnson, a tattooed tough guy with a surprising soft side, raised a bottle of barbecue sauce in acknowledgment before slathering it on a plate of steaming hot ribs.

"Feel free to use my new glaze while we're gone," Colt added, nodding toward the saucepan on the stove.

Jack bit back a sarcastic remark, marching out of the kitchen before he said something he'd regret.

To his chagrin, Colt continued to blabber about menu changes as they strode across the town square toward The Calendar Café, a bakery and coffee shop that served as the town gathering place.

After drawing in a deep breath, Jack exhaled slowly, watching his breath escape in a hazy white cloud. The frigid night air helped him keep his cool.

While he didn't blame Colt for his enthusiasm, Jack knew the danger of blind ambition. He'd watched it tear his family apart. Growing up, they'd barely had enough money to make ends meet, but they had each other. And for a time, that had been enough.

Unbidden, his thoughts flew to the Christmas card buried beneath a stack of junk mail. In the professional photograph, his entire family gathered in front of a grandiose mansion wearing matching red turtlenecks, most likely cashmere. Although the rift between Jack and his parents had been going on for years, they'd kept him on their mailing list. Probably to rub salt in the wound.

Not only did it pain Jack to see the garish display of wealth, but he couldn't bear the depressing reminder that all four of his brothers had followed in his father's footsteps, right down to their expensive Italian leather loafers. Unfortunately, the tension between Jack and his parents had strained the whole family. And although Jack didn't hold anything against his siblings, he barely spoke to them anymore.

Except for Lucy. Fresh out of college, and the only girl, she still saw the world with rose-colored glasses. In fact, she optimistically tried to reunite Jack with their parents at every available opportunity. He often wondered if she'd give up if he told her the reason for the division. But out of love and concern for her, he kept the ugly truth to himself.

Absentmindedly, Jack dug his hand inside his coat pocket, grazing his cell phone. He expected a call from her any day now announcing her annual holiday visit.

Although their parents lived in the neighboring town of Primrose Valley, Lucy never missed spending a few days in Poppy Creek with Jack to kick off the Christmas season. Their itinerary usually consisted of gorging themselves on too many sugar cookies while binge-watching Christmas movies. One year, she'd even talked him into wearing an eggnog face mask while they sang along with Bing Crosby and Fred Astaire in their favorite film, *Holiday Inn*. But he drew the line at painting his toenails with candy cane stripes.

Smiling at the memory, Jack felt the tension lift from his shoulders. No matter what went wrong in his world—even an overzealous sous-chef wreaking havoc on his diner—a visit from his sister set everything right again.

In truth, he didn't think he could survive the holidays without it.

*a*s Jack pushed through the front door of The Calendar Café, a barrage of warm air greeted him.

Half the town of Poppy Creek appeared to be crammed in between the overflowing pastry cases and enormous open-hearth fireplace. After removing his wool coat, Jack pushed the sleeves of his flannel shirt up to his elbows as he scanned the crowd.

His gaze rested on Frank Barrie and his fiancée, Beverly, canoodling at a table in the center of the room. Jack's lips twitched at the uncommon sight. He still couldn't get used to seeing the town curmudgeon with his arm around the sweet, soft-spoken librarian. As someone stubbornly set in his ways, Jack had a hard time processing the drastic transformation.

Seated next to them at the table, Luke and Colt's mother, Maggie, clutched a plaid scrapbook Jack instantly recognized as the Christmas Calendar. While the original version had been destroyed last year, the reproduction looked identical, right down to the gold foil lettering across the front. The pages inside were filled with all twenty-five festive tasks laid out by Cassie's late grandparents before they passed away—a precious family heirloom that evoked a tiny pang of envy in Jack's heart.

Growing up, Jack's family hadn't owned many possessions. And the ones they *had* owned were promptly upgraded when his father's real estate business took off. Jack had managed to save only one keepsake—the cast-iron skillet that had kickstarted his love of cooking comfort food.

"Hey, you two! You made it." The bright, cheerful voice interrupted Jack's thoughts.

Penny Heart rushed to welcome them, throwing her arms around Colt's neck before kissing him as though they'd been separated for several months.

Jack averted his gaze. Nearly everyone he knew seemed to be dating, engaged, or married. And nothing amplified his single status quite like being surrounded by couples in love, especially during the holidays. After all, he couldn't exactly kiss himself under the mistletoe, now could he?

"There they are!" Eliza Carter, Cassie's best friend and business partner, gestured toward them, snaking her way through the throng. Her fiancé, Grant, followed on her heels, their son, Ben, lagging behind them.

"Luke and Cassie are in the kitchen," Eliza told them breathlessly, her huge chocolate-brown eyes dancing with delight. "He's distracting her under the guise of hanging a new spice rack he made for us. I can't wait to see the look on her face when she sees everyone!"

"And the Calendar," Penny added, sounding equally excited.

"I wanna see Aunt Cassie, too." Ben tugged on his father's arm.

As Grant glanced down at his son, a crease appeared in his forehead. Although on the smaller side for an eight-year-old, Ben wasn't exactly a little kid anymore, either.

Grant scanned the room, presumably looking for a chair Ben could stand on, but they were all occupied.

"Don't worry, I've got you covered." With minimal effort, Jack hoisted Ben onto his broad shoulders. "How's that?"

"Whoa! I can see everything from up here," Ben gushed, clearly impressed with his new vantage point.

"Welcome to my world," Jack chuckled. At six four, he was used to the unencumbered view.

"He's not too heavy?" Grant asked.

"Nah. I barely even notice him." The eldest of six, Jack wasn't a stranger to kids crawling all over him like a jungle gym. And if he were honest, he missed being needed by his younger siblings. For years, he'd been the one in charge while his parents each worked two jobs to put food on the table.

"They're coming!" Eliza squealed, bouncing on her toes.

A hush settled over the crowd, all eyes glued to the swinging door that led to the kitchen as Luke and Cassie emerged. Luke covered his wife's eyes with both hands as he carefully guided her around the long counter and display cases filled with tempting desserts, of which Jack had sampled every single one.

"What's going on?" Cassie laughed, her hands stretched out before her as she took hesitant steps forward.

"It's a surprise." Luke paused at the edge of the round table where his mother sat with Frank and Beverly and slowly lowered his hands.

As Cassie's gaze fell on the Christmas Calendar, in all its newly restored glory, she gasped in surprise. "How did you—"

"Mom and Beverly did most of the work," Luke admitted, casting an appreciative glance in their direction.

"We tried to recreate it as close to the original as possible." Maggie's hazel eyes glistened as she handed it to her daughter-in-law.

Accepting it gingerly, Cassie whispered, "I can't believe it."

"Mom even found a recipe card for your grandmother's mince pie written in her own handwriting," Luke told her, his voice thick with emotion.

"I—I don't know what to say." Cassie blinked back tears as her gaze flitted from Luke to the faces of her dear friends, who all looked on with fondness.

"You don't need to say anything, sweetheart." Maggie smiled warmly. "We all love you dearly and wanted to make this Christmas as special as your first one in Poppy Creek. In a way, the Calendar is meaningful to all of us, since it brought you to our little town and into our lives."

"Tell her the best part," Eliza practically shouted in her eagerness.

Maggie chuckled. "I'll let Luke do the honors."

"We added some blank pages." Luke gazed at his wife with tender affection. "In case we want to start a few of our own traditions."

Cassie reached for his hand. "Oh, Luke, I love that idea."

As Luke pulled her in for a quick kiss, the hollow feeling in Jack's chest expanded. He wondered what it would be like to have someone by his side to not only share in special traditions, but make new ones. Suddenly, although surrounded by people, Jack had never felt more alone.

Still wrapped in Luke's arms, Cassie addressed the group, her green eyes shimmering. "Thank you all. I can't tell you how much it means to me. Before I came to Poppy Creek, I never imagined how drastically my life would change. You didn't just welcome me into your town, you welcomed me into your hearts. And because of you, I now have a family. A large, boisterous family who's thankfully very fond of coffee and calorie-rich desserts."

At that, everyone chuckled.

As the crowd gathered around the newlyweds, doling out hugs and admiring the Calendar, Jack remained near the back of the room, mulling over his conflicting thoughts.

While he wholeheartedly agreed with Cassie's sentiments— the people of Poppy Creek were his family, too—he couldn't deny the dull ache in his heart.

But he had no clue what to do about it.

❄

*T*he rustle of worn pages harmonized with the soothing hum of waves lapping against the shoreline as Kat immersed herself in *A Christmas Carol*. Reading the beloved classic had become a tradition every December 1 after decorating the house with Fern. Even though she knew nearly every word by heart, she found the redemptive tale comforting. During the toughest time of the year, she relished the hopeful reminder that even Scrooge turned his life around.

"Knock, knock."

Kat glanced up from her lounging position on the bed to find Fern standing in the doorway with a tray of hot chocolate and her mouthwatering Milagros. "I thought you might be in need of a bedtime snack."

Kat sat up a little straighter and laid the open book across her lap. "Thank you. That sounds lovely."

Fern slid the tray onto the nightstand, and Kat inhaled the scent of rich dark chocolate and sweet cinnamon.

"One of my favorite stories." The mattress creaked as Fern perched on the edge of the bed, plucking the thin book from its resting place. "This is a beautiful copy." She caressed the red leather binding and gold-embossed lettering.

"A thrift store find, if you can believe it." Kat eagerly reached for the steaming mug of cocoa, smiling as the smooth ceramic warmed her cold fingertips. Although the temperature often reached the low fifties along the California coast in early December, she liked to crack her bedroom window to savor the serene sound of the ocean.

"You know my favorite part of the story?" Fern asked.

"The ending?" Kat guessed, taking a sip. The thick, syrupy liquid slid down her throat, followed by a hint of spice. The dash of cayenne pepper and cinnamon lent Fern's hot chocolate an extra burst of flavor that other recipes lacked.

Fern shook her head, flipping backward a few pages, while keeping one finger in the spine so she didn't lose Kat's place. "My favorite part is when Scrooge sees Jacob Marley and accuses him of being a moldy piece of cheese." She chuckled softly before turning back to Kat's spot, gently laying the book facedown on the faded quilt. "We all do that, don't we?"

"Do what?" Cradling the mug in her palm, Kat nibbled on the sugary treat.

"When there's something we're too afraid to face, we pretend it doesn't exist."

Even though they were discussing a work of fiction, Kat's thoughts wandered to the envelope tucked in the bottom drawer of her nightstand. And she had a feeling Fern knew that it would. The older woman had a special knack for seeing right through a person's carefully erected walls to their innermost secrets.

"I suppose we do...." She set the half-eaten cookie back on the plate, no longer hungry.

"Did I ever tell you the meaning behind my name?"

"Fern?"

"Fernanda. It means *brave journey*. I've always thought that was fitting, considering the path my life has taken."

"I wish I could be as strong as you," Kat admitted with genuine longing. She kept most of her past locked in the deep recesses of her mind so she didn't have to face the painful memories.

"Want to know my secret?" Fern asked in a conspiratorial whisper. "I put one foot in front of the other and wait for God to open a door."

"You make it sound so easy."

"Easy? Have you seen how big my feet are? It's a wonder I don't trip all over myself." She laughed—rich and warm like her delicious hot chocolate—and Kat cracked a smile.

How she could find joy and humor in the face of all the sorrow she'd experienced, Kat would never know. Not for the first time, Kat wished Fern was her mother, instead of the less-than-stellar role model she'd been given at birth. "And what if God doesn't open a door?"

"Oh, mija, He always does. But sometimes, it's not the one we think it will be." She leaned forward and lovingly brushed aside a wayward strand of Kat's wild red hair. "Now, don't stay up too late."

After bidding her good night, Fern shuffled across the thread-bare carpet and through the doorway.

Kat waited for her footsteps to disappear down the hallway before she slid open the bottom drawer of her nightstand. With hesitant hands, she retrieved a thin white envelope from beneath a stack of books.

The letter, addressed to her mother, Helena Bennet, care of Hope Hideaway, was postmarked over four months ago from a small town several hours inland called Poppy Creek.

Slowly, Kat slipped the single sheet of paper from the envelope, along with a wallet-size photograph. Her stomach twisted as she gazed into the bright coppery eyes so full of life and light.

When she'd first glimpsed the photo, she'd assumed it was her mother, taken decades before her tragic death. The young woman had the same striking eyes, auburn hair, and delicate features. When she'd gazed at the beautiful, carefree smile, Kat had broken down in tears, painfully reminded of the mother she'd tried so desperately to forget.

Then, she'd read the neat, sloping penmanship, and her entire world had shattered in the span of a single breath.

Dear Helena,

I've debated contacting you since you've made it clear you don't want any communication between us. But I've recently discovered I have a half sister, and I'm hoping you'll pass along a message. I would love the chance to meet her, if she's willing. I've enclosed a photo, and she can find me at the return address. I took over Dad's antiques store when he passed away.

Respectfully,
Penny Heart

Kat swallowed against the lump of emotion lodged in her throat. Like Scrooge, she'd tried to explain away the unwelcome reality that she had a half sister—it was a mistake or a cruel joke. But in her heart, she didn't doubt the truth of the letter. Knowing her reckless and capricious mother all too well, the possibility of another family—another life—wasn't far-fetched. In fact, she had vague memories of her mother mourning the loss of a stunning brooch, crafted from emeralds, rubies, and diamonds, given to her by a man named Timothy Heart—the only man Helena ever referred to with any glimmer of warmth or affection.

Putting the pieces together, Kat realized Helena hadn't simply left a piece of jewelry behind—she'd left a child, a sister Kat never knew existed.

When Fern gave Kat the envelope—since her mother had passed away several years before its delivery—she hadn't pried about the contents. Part of Kat wanted to confide in Fern, but then she'd have to face complicated emotions she'd long repressed. In the end, she'd pretended the letter, and her sister, didn't exist. They remained a part of her mother's past, where Helena had clearly wanted to keep them.

As Kat folded the note and slid it back inside the envelope along with the photograph, her thoughts drifted to the bejeweled brooch. While her mother rarely spoke about her life before moving to Starcross Cove, she'd frequently lamented leaving the prized possession behind, presumably because it must have been worth a small fortune—a pawnshop gold mine that could feed her many addictions for years.

A small fortune...

Kat bolted upright in bed as an impulsive idea gripped her.

CHAPTER 3

After rising from his kneeling position on the cobbled sidewalk, Jack wiped his chalk-covered palms on his jeans, surveying his handiwork. He'd begrudgingly added *espresso molasses brisket* to the sandwich board featuring the day's specials.

Long-term, they'd have to come up with a solution for their differing visions for the diner, but for now, Jack decided to let his friend explore his culinary creativity, even if it did attract the wrong clientele. In the last two days alone, he'd had one patron ask if their potatoes were humanely boiled—whatever that meant —and another insisted her coffee mug be cleaned multiple times because it was "filthy." He'd tried to explain the tiny flecks on the speckled pottery were a part of the design, but in the end, he'd given her a plain white mug to placate her concerns.

Overall, he didn't mind tourists and understood they brought beneficial cash flow into the community, but he didn't agree with Mayor Burns's high-handed marketing methods or compromising their small-town values. In fact, most visitors came to Poppy Creek to escape the doldrums of city life in favor of a more leisurely pace and peaceful mindset.

Glancing around the town square, Jack felt his chest fill with pride. The Western-style buildings with their shiplap, stone, and brick facades evoked their historic roots harkening back to gold rush days. Stores like Mac's Mercantile and Sadie's Sweet Shop, while updated for modern consumers, still maintained their original whimsy and charm, accentuated by old-fashioned decorations like evergreen garlands and holly wreaths. For decades, all four streets surrounding the town square had been occupied with mom-and-pop shops, not chain stores or conglomerations. And Jack hoped it would stay that way.

The slam of a car door drew his attention across the center lawn, and he stood, transfixed, as afternoon sunlight streamed through the branches of a towering oak tree alighting on the woman's fiery red hair, setting it ablaze.

He watched her take tentative steps toward Thistle & Thorn —the town's quirky antiques store—her long hair and fringed scarf fluttering in the crisp breeze.

Startled by a vibration in his back pocket, Jack scrambled for his phone. "Hello?" Unable to tear his gaze from the enigmatic newcomer, he answered without glancing at the caller ID.

"Flap Jack! What kind of boring greeting is that?"

His lips quirked as his sister's playful indignation emanated through the speakers. "Hey, Lucy Bug," he drawled warmly using her nickname. "It's about time you called. Are you on your way?"

A gust of wind lifted the stranger's scarf from her shoulders, and it fluttered toward the ground.

"Hang on, Luce. I'll call you right back." Stuffing the phone back inside his pocket, he trotted across the lawn and plucked her scarf from a pile of leaves. "Excuse me, miss. You dropped this."

She didn't appear to hear him as she stood stock-still in front of Thistle & Thorn, her brow furrowed as though debating whether or not she wanted to enter.

"Miss?" he tried again.

Oblivious to the world around her, the woman hesitated a few feet from the entrance.

Something about her pensive expression gave Jack pause, but he'd come too far to give up now.

Besides, for reasons he couldn't articulate, he desperately wanted to meet her.

❄

*H*er heartbeat thrumming erratically, Kat stared at the worn brass knob, but couldn't bring herself to turn it. Suddenly, what lay beyond the bright teal door felt all too real.

What had she been thinking coming here? Did she really expect Penny to still have the brooch, let alone agree to sell it and split the proceeds with her? After all, apart from the whole having-the-same-mother thing, they were complete strangers. And Kat had every intention of keeping it that way.

Forming any kind of relationship with the woman who happened to be the spitting image of their degenerate mother was out of the question. For all Kat knew, the two women could share more than their outward appearance. Addiction was often hereditary, and Kat had already watched her mother self-destruct. She couldn't handle any more heartache.

As she reconsidered her impulsive plan, she felt a faint tap on her shoulder. Instinctively acting on several years of self-defense training, she grabbed the large, burly hand and stepped backward swiftly. With a sharp, forceful twist, she pinned the man's arm behind his back.

"Easy!" he howled. "That's my favorite limb."

Realizing what she'd done, she blushed and immediately released her hold. "I'm sorry, I— You caught me by surprise."

"I can see that." He rubbed his shoulder, his vivid blue eyes sparkling with a mixture of surprise and amusement.

"I'm sorry about your arm. I hope I didn't hurt it too badly."

"No worries. I still have the left one." He grinned good-naturedly, and Kat couldn't help returning his smile. Normally, she avoided talking to strange men, but this one exuded warmth and kindness, instantly putting her at ease.

"Word of advice," she said with a lighthearted tone. "It's not safe to sneak up on people. I could have broken your arm."

"Are you sure you didn't?" He cradled it with an exaggerated grimace, and Kat's smile widened, enjoying his playful sense of humor.

"Where'd you learn a move like that?" he asked.

"I teach Krav Maga, a combat technique used by Israeli soldiers. Although, my classes are mainly for self-defense."

As he surveyed her petite five-six frame he appeared genuinely impressed. "Remind me to stay on your good side."

"Who says you're on it?" she teased, surprised to find herself flirting with this man. She didn't flirt—ever.

"Does it help that I rescued your scarf from a pile of diabolical leaves?"

As her gaze fell on the houndstooth fabric in his grasp, her hand flew to her throat. "Oh! I didn't even realize I'd dropped it. Thank you." As she reached for it, their fingers grazed, and a pleasant warmth crept up her arm. Had he felt the same sensation?

Feeling like a romantic comedy cliché, she hastily wrapped the scarf around her neck and prepared to duck inside the antiques store, if only to escape the unsettling effect he had on her. She'd never experienced this type of instant connection before and it didn't sit well. Once she got what she came for, she'd be on her way home, with zero plans to ever return.

"Can I buy you a cup of coffee? There's a great café right down the street. Cassie has a knack for knowing exactly what kind of coffee you'll like. And Eliza's desserts are legendary."

Kat blinked. Had he just asked her out? "Oh, um... thank you,

RACHAEL BLOOME

but I won't be in town long. I'm hoping to find something at the antiques store, then I'm heading back home."

Was it her imagination or did he look disappointed?

"I'm sorry to hear that. Apart from the dislocated shoulder, it was a pleasure meeting you…" He trailed off with a questioning glance.

"Kat Bennet," she answered against her better judgment. What had gotten into her? She never gave strangers her name, let alone her last name, too. It felt oddly formal and unnecessary, as though she wanted to disassociate herself from her sister as much as possible, even though this man had no way of suspecting any connection whatsoever.

"I'm Jack Gardener. It was nice to meet you, Bennet. I hope you find what you're looking for."

And with that, he turned and strolled down the street, leaving her bizarrely breathless.

Rattled by the exchange and the unexpected yet pleasant way he used her last name instead of her first, she pushed open the door and quickly stepped inside as though fleeing the scene of a crime.

Immediately, the scent of dried lavender and aged leather greeted her, accompanied by the sultry crooning of Ella Fitzgerald's "White Christmas" emanating from a crackling gramophone.

"Hi! Welcome to Thistle & Thorn. What can I help you find today?"

Like a vivid apparition, a younger version of her mother approached from across the room, her friendly smile doing little to assuage Kat's turbulent heartbeat or flood of unwelcome memories rushing to the surface. For a brief moment, she closed her eyes, afraid the burning sensation was a precursor for unwanted—and embarrassing—tears.

Keep it together, Kat, she chided herself. *You have to do this. For Fern.*

22

"I—I'm looking for a vintage brooch. But first, there's something I need to tell you."

"Oh?" The statuesque redhead tilted her head to the side in curiosity.

Taking a deep breath, Kat released her confession in a slow, shaky exhale. "I'm... your sister."

CHAPTER 4

*K*at's pulse slowed until it nearly halted altogether as she waited for a response.

"Wh-what?" Penny's color drained, her shock evident.

Comparing the two of them side by side, it was no wonder she had difficulty believing Kat's claim. Besides their red hair—of which Penny's appeared more auburn—they had little in common.

"I'm Kat Bennet. Helena Bennet's daughter. And your half sister."

Penny sank onto a plum-velvet chaise lounge, her pallid complexion turning puce.

Softening, Kat empathized with her stunned reaction. Although Penny knew of her existence, after months without a single word of correspondence, her impromptu visit had clearly come as a surprise.

Glancing around the quirky shop, she spotted a small refreshment table serving tea and cookies. She quickly filled one of the small paper cups with the hot liquid that smelled of orange zest and cloves and brought it over to her sister, gently sitting beside her.

Penny accepted it with trembling hands and slowly took a sip. "I can't believe it," she murmured over the brim. "When I didn't hear from you after a while, I gave up hope." She turned to Kat, her eyes glistening. "I'm so glad you came." Mindful not to spill her tea, Penny slipped her arms around Kat's shoulders, hugging her tightly.

Uncomfortable with displays of affection, especially from strangers, Kat kept both arms glued to her sides, sitting rigid on the tufted cushion.

Pulling away, Penny wiped her damp cheek with her free hand and asked, "Did Helena ever tell you about me?"

"No, she didn't. She never talked about her old life." Kat cringed at her use of the past tense. She'd wanted to ease into the news about Helena's death, not spring it on her sister with an offhand comment.

But Penny didn't seem to notice, still in a daze. "I can't get over the fact that you're actually here! How long can you stay?"

"I... I can't stay long." Chewing her bottom lip, Kat struggled with how to explain her visit. "I'm actually here because I need your help."

"Anything," Penny said quickly.

Kat blinked, surprised by her eagerness to help, considering they barely knew each other. "I'm looking for something that belonged to our mother. A brooch crafted out of diamonds, emeralds, and rubies. It looks like a sprig of mistletoe. I suppose it's a long shot that you still have it but I'm desperate."

"Desperate?"

"Hope Hideaway, a women's shelter where I live and work, is on the verge of closing. I thought that maybe, if you still had the brooch, you might be willing to sell it and split the money with me. My half would go toward saving the shelter."

"I see..." Penny's slender eyebrows knit together.

Kat held her breath, her heart beating in short, agonizing bursts for what felt like hours. This was a mistake. She shouldn't

25

have sprung this on Penny—it was too much for one person to process in a matter of minutes. Riddled with regret, Kat leaped from the chaise lounge. "I'm so sorry. I shouldn't be here. I should never have asked you to—"

"It's not that," Penny said hastily, scrambling to her feet. "I want to help. You can have the brooch, as long as it's okay with Helena. Even though she left it with my father, I don't really feel like it's mine to give away. But if she's okay with you selling it, you can use every last dime for the shelter."

For a moment, Kat stood speechless. She hadn't expected such selfless generosity. She also hadn't expected spilling the news about Helena's death to be so difficult. Although the words rested on the tip of her tongue, she couldn't bring herself to say them out loud, knowing they would incite questions she wasn't ready to answer. "Thank you," she said softly, resolving to tell Penny about their mother at another time. "I can't tell you how much that means to me... to the shelter."

"I'm happy to help. Truly. Let me flip the Closed sign on the front door, then we'll head upstairs."

"Upstairs?"

"I live in the apartment above the shop. The brooch is with my dad's things."

Recalling the portion in Penny's letter about her father's passing, she offered, "I was sorry to hear about your dad. Were you close?"

"Closer than close." Penny's eyes glimmered with warmth. "He was my best friend."

Unexpectedly, tears welled in Kat's eyes and she dismissed them with a sharp exhale. Oh, what she wouldn't give to have one loving, dependable parent to speak of with such fondness. But a child didn't get to choose that sort of thing. They simply had to play with the cards they were dealt. Or in her case, shuffle those particular cards to the bottom of the deck where they belonged.

Kat followed Penny past a thick brocade curtain into a

disheveled storage room, then up a narrow staircase, her nerves mounting with each step.

Already emotionally drained from the experience, Kat couldn't wait to secure the brooch and head back home, where she could leave the entire ordeal behind her for good.

*L*ost in his thoughts, Jack didn't even notice the black smoke curling from the cast-iron skillet.

"Whoa! You're taking charred chicken to a whole other level." Yanking on an oven mitt, Colt quickly removed the skillet from the heat and switched off the burner.

Snapping to attention, Jack jammed on a lid before the murky cloud set off the smoke detector. "Sorry, I don't know what happened."

Okay, so that wasn't technically true. He'd been daydreaming about the enigmatic stranger who'd nearly broken his arm. But he wasn't about to admit that to Colt. He also wasn't going to admit that he'd asked her out after a grand total of five minutes. Even if he did, his friend probably wouldn't believe him. When it came to dating, Jack wasn't exactly known for taking chances.

"Don't tell me Vick and I need to start babysitting you around the stove," Colt teased.

Jack rolled his eyes. "If anyone needs babysitting, it's you. Every time I turn my back, you've whipped up a new recipe."

"That reminds me. I wanted to talk to you about doing a special holiday menu."

Saved by his vibrating phone, Jack eagerly slipped it out of his back pocket. "Hold that thought." Glancing at the caller ID, he realized he'd forgotten to return his sister's call. "Hey, Luce." He pressed the phone to his ear as he stepped into his cramped office at the back of the kitchen. "Sorry I didn't call back. I got side-tracked. How long ago did you leave LA?"

"About an hour ago." Her voice crackled in her car's Bluetooth speakers.

"Great! So I'll see you for a late dinner. What would you like? I'll make you anything you want. Except for sushi." He chuckled, recalling how her tastes had evolved since she moved to Los Angeles after college to pursue her dream of designing movie sets for Hollywood.

"That's what I've been trying to tell you..." She trailed off, and Jack glanced at the phone, checking their connection when he didn't hear anything for several seconds.

"Luce?" he prompted, reclining in his battered leather chair. He thought about pushing aside the mountain of paperwork to prop up his feet, but he stretched them under the desk instead.

She released a crestfallen sigh. "I can't come this year."

"What?" He bolted upright, banging his knee against the sharp corner of an open drawer. Suppressing a groan, he rubbed the sore spot. "What do you mean you can't come?"

"I want to, but Mom got it into her head that she wants to throw a huge party on Christmas Day and needs my help to plan it."

"You don't say." He couldn't help the bitter edge that crept into his voice.

Accustomed to being in the middle of their feud, Lucy ignored his sardonic droll. "Why don't you come to Primrose Valley for Christmas this year? It's less than an hour away."

"You know I can't do that. Besides, Mom's elaborate parties aren't really my thing."

"What about wassailing? The whole family is going. You used to love it when we were kids."

Closing his eyes, Jack pressed his fingertips to his temple as memories of their family caroling tradition came rushing back. They used to borrow Victorian-era costumes from Sylvia Carter, the local theater director, and carol around town, serving hot cider—classically called wassail—and homemade sugar cookies.

Since both of their parents loved to sing, the skill had been passed down to Jack and his siblings. He was surprised to learn they'd maintained the tradition all these years. Although, he imagined their private chef made the wassail these days. And the cookies probably came from some pricey boutique bakery.

When he didn't respond right away, Lucy pleaded, "Please come, Flap Jack. Everyone misses you, especially Mom and Dad."

He had to snort at that one. Her statement oozed irony considering they were the reason he'd been alienated from nearly his entire family. "Sorry, Luce. You know I can't. Are you sure Mom needs you for the whole month?" Only a few days into December, they still had weeks to plan a Christmas party.

"You know how she is. If her event doesn't rival a White House gala, it's not worth throwing."

Oh, he knew all too well. And he hated that their mother's pretentious extravagance had usurped their time together. "Well, if anything changes, let me know. I'll be here. And I'll save *Holiday Inn* in case you can come after all."

She laughed although it lacked some of its usual mirth. "Deal."

Silence filled the speaker, and Jack got the sense she had more to say.

"Something else on your mind?" he asked.

"No, nothing," she said unconvincingly, bidding him a hasty goodbye.

After the call ended, Jack hung his head in his hands, his heart heavy.

Maybe he should have fought harder to keep the tradition of her annual visit alive, but he'd learned a long time ago that competing with his parents always ended badly.

At least, it had when it came to his ex.

CHAPTER 5

*U*pon entering Penny's home, Kat immediately noted the warm, cozy atmosphere. Old-fashioned Christmas decorations like fresh cedar garlands and vintage ornaments complemented the assortment of antique furniture and collectibles.

"It's in here." Penny motioned toward a door Kat hadn't noticed. Painted the same porcelain-white as the walls, it blended seamlessly into the surroundings.

As she crossed the plush art deco rug, Kat yelped, taken aback as something waddled past her. Hardly able to believe her eyes, she gaped at a large Russian tortoise. Or rather, at its backside as it shuffled toward an enormous custom-built enclosure partially hidden by potted plants.

"Don't worry," Penny said with a smile. "That's Chip. He wouldn't hurt a fly. Well, he *might* if he could catch one." She laughed, and Kat breathed a little easier.

"You have a pet tortoise?"

"We're more like roommates. And he's the one in charge."

Kat grinned, suppressing the urge to stroke his leathery head. She'd always wanted a pet—a dog, specifically. But Fern had a policy against furry animals, since you never knew if someone would be allergic.

"This used to be my dad's bedroom and office," Penny explained, giving the door a firm nudge with her hip. "I've kept it exactly as he left it."

Kat followed her into the modest space, momentarily mesmerized by the wall of bookshelves, nautical trinkets, and stunning brass telescope on a vintage mahogany tripod. "Your dad must've been quite the adventurer."

"In his own way, he was." Penny dropped to her knees and reached beneath the wrought iron bed frame, retrieving a small wooden chest.

Kat's pulse spiked. This was it. The entire reason she'd come here. Her only hope for saving the shelter resided inside the dusty box.

Penny flipped open the lid and a flicker of surprise darted across her face.

"What's wrong?" Kat took a step closer, her heartbeat stuttering.

"It's gone."

"What do you mean *gone*? Like, it's been stolen?"

"Not stolen." An unexpected smile curling her lips, Penny plucked a folded square of paper from inside. "There's a clue."

"What do you mean? A clue for what?"

With a fond, wistful expression, Penny explained, "When I was a kid, my dad would set up elaborate treasure hunts in the apartment. He'd hide an object, then leave me clues, often riddles, to help me find it. He must have planned one for my first Christmas home from college. Before he died..." Her voice fell away in a soft whisper, and for a long moment, she didn't speak, merely staring into the distance.

"What does it say?" Kat asked gently, balancing her eagerness with empathy.

Blinking a few times, as though slowly returning to the

present, Penny unfolded the note and read it out loud. "'The stars wait for no man, and neither does the sun. Once you think it's over, it's really just begun.'" Her hands dropped to her lap, a puzzled expression clouding her features.

Kat frowned. "Do you have any idea what it means?"

"I'm afraid not. The clues weren't usually this difficult. I suppose Dad figured I could handle more challenging ones in college." She smiled again, but Kat didn't find the situation amusing. She didn't have time for games.

Pacing the floor, she furrowed her brow in thought. "If we put our heads together, surely we can solve it. Would you mind reading it again?"

Penny obliged, but hearing the words a second time—or even a third—didn't lend any more clarity.

Kat ran her fingers through her hair in exasperation. "We'll never find the brooch at this rate."

"We'll figure it out," Penny said cheerfully, rising to her feet. "We just need to give it some time. And perhaps some food and a good night's sleep."

"Oh, I didn't plan on staying," Kat reminded her quickly. "I didn't book a hotel or pack a bag."

"I can call Trudy at the Morning Glory Inn and see if she has a room available," Penny offered. "And I have several racks of vintage clothing downstairs. I'm sure we can find something that will fit. As far as bath and beauty products go, the inn provides lovely hospitality kits. And anything Trudy doesn't have you can borrow from me."

Kat's frown deepened. First of all, she couldn't afford to spend the night at a run-down motel, let alone an inn. Secondly, spending more time with Penny would only complicate the situation. Not to mention give her sister more opportunity to bring up the one subject that was off-limits—their mother. "I don't know...."

"One night," Penny persisted. "I'm sure we'll have the clue figured out by this time tomorrow."

"I guess one night would be okay," she relented out of desperation. While less than ideal, her credit card could cover the room charge.

Finding the brooch needed to be the priority above everything else.

"Hooray!" Penny clapped her hands in excitement, skipping toward the door. "I'll call Trudy."

Kat wrenched her phone out of her coat pocket. Somehow, she'd have to inform Fern she wouldn't be coming home tonight without revealing her secret mission. No reason to get her hopes up in case the plan didn't come to fruition.

And based on the latest wrinkle, there was an extremely good chance it wouldn't.

*A*fter taking a few minutes to clear his head, Jack returned to the kitchen, determined not to let his sister's bad news affect the rest of the day.

"You're never going to believe this." His tone awestruck, Colt stuffed his phone in the back pocket of his jeans.

"What's up?"

"I just got a call from Penny."

"We should alert the *Poppy Creek Press*," Jack teased.

"Har-har," Colt said wryly. "It's *what* the call was about that's newsworthy." He paused theatrically as Jack grabbed a russet potato and peeler.

"Spill it, Davis. And while you're at it…" He nodded toward the cutting board.

Colt grabbed a chef's knife and waited for Jack to hand him the first peeled potato. "Penny's long-lost sister showed up today," he announced in a hushed tone, glancing over his shoulder to see if anyone else in the kitchen had overheard him.

The peeler slipped from Jack's grasp, nearly taking off a chunk of his thumb. "Penny's sister?"

"Crazy, right? After months of no response, she showed up out of the blue."

"What do you know about her?" Jack couldn't contain his curiosity. She had to be the woman he'd encountered in front of Thistle & Thorn earlier that afternoon. And if the two women were related, there might be a slim chance he would see more of her after all.

"Not much. Penny couldn't talk long. But she sounded a little disappointed."

"How so?"

"She said her sister planned on leaving town today. Apparently, she only came to pick up a piece of jewelry that belonged to their mother and didn't seem interested in getting to know Penny at all. Strange, right?"

Jack let Colt's words sink in, disheartened on Penny's behalf. And his own, if he were honest. He'd felt an instant connection to Kat, but based on this new information, his first impression might have been wrong. "Has she left already?"

"I guess there was a hiccup in her original plan, and she's staying another day or two. They're stopping by the diner in a few minutes."

This time, the peeler made contact with his flesh. "Ouch!" Jack flicked his wrist, waiting for the sting to pass. Luckily, he hadn't drawn blood.

"Are *you* trying to add something new to the menu now?" Colt smirked once he'd made sure Jack hadn't seriously hurt himself. "Because I've always thought we could use more finger food."

"Hilarious," Jack muttered, sucking on his offended finger. "Why are they coming here?"

"For a late lunch."

"I'm curious, what made her decide to stay longer?"

"I don't know all the details. But it sounds like they couldn't find what she was looking for, so she's sticking around town until they do."

Still licking his wound, Jack couldn't decide how he felt about the news. On one hand, he was anxious to see her again. On the other hand, it was much safer for his heart if he didn't.

He'd already fallen for a woman who cared more about possessions than people.

And he couldn't risk making the same mistake twice.

CHAPTER 6

*G*nawing her bottom lip, Kat paced the musty bedroom, waiting for Fern to answer the phone. Her gaze kept drifting to the empty box and perplexing riddle. Definitely not how she'd expected the day to go.

"Hi, mija. I'm just starting the tamales. When will you be home?"

"I'm afraid I won't be back tonight after all."

"Oh?" Despite her inflection, she didn't sound surprised.

"The special errand I mentioned earlier is taking longer than I'd anticipated."

"You mean the top secret one you won't tell me about?"

"Yep, that's the one." Kat smiled at the older woman's teasing lilt.

"Should I send you a few things? A change of clothes, perhaps?"

"No, that's all right. I should be home by tomorrow night at the latest. I can make do until then."

"Are you sure?"

"I'm sure. But thank you." Kat definitely didn't want to explain what had brought her to Poppy Creek. Although, she sometimes

36

wondered if Fern could read minds and knew her thoughts even before she did.

"Have fun, mija. I can't wait to hear all about your mysterious adventure when you get back."

Feeling comforted—as she usually did after talking to Fern— Kat bid her goodbye and ended the call.

A second later, Penny pranced through the doorway, a grin splashed across her face. "Guess what? Trudy has a room available! And she said there's no charge since my family is her family."

"Oh, I couldn't impose like that," Kat insisted, despite her empty bank account.

"Good luck talking her out of it. She can be pretty stubborn," Penny said warmly. "Before you check in, let's get something to eat. I'm famished and there's someone I want you to meet."

For some unknown reason, Kat's thoughts immediately flew to the man she'd assaulted on the street earlier. Jack was his name, wasn't it? Either way, she had no idea why the image of his benevolent blue eyes flashed into her mind. Or why her stomach fluttered the instant it did. "I am a little hungry...." She'd brought a couple of Fern's cookies for the drive, but that's all she'd had to eat since her cup of black coffee and dry toast that morning.

Penny spun toward the door, then froze, her face brightening with a sudden recollection. "Wait! First, we need to find you some clothes."

"That really isn't necessary...." Although a generous offer, she'd already settled on washing her undergarments in the sink and hanging them to dry by a furnace or fireplace, assuming her room had one.

"Don't be silly! Half the fun of my job is helping people put together beautiful outfits. And I just got in a gorgeous peacoat in the most stunning shade of kelly green that'll go perfectly with your red hair. You'll look like Christmas personified."

Kat ran a hand over the faded black wool of her shapeless

overcoat, contrasting it with the shimmering vintage shawl wrapped around her sister's tall, willowy frame.

"Maybe the coat," she relented. "If it's not too expensive. I don't have much room in my budget for new clothes." Or a stick of gum, she thought morosely.

Penny placed one hand on her hip, her copper eyes twinkling. "I see you're going to be a tough nut to crack. Are you this bad at accepting Christmas presents?"

Kat hesitated. Truthfully, she'd only ever exchanged gifts with Fern. "I'm sorry. I guess I'm not used to strangers being so generous."

She realized her blunder a second too late. Sure, the term was technically accurate, but calling her sister a stranger sounded harsh even to her own ears. How would she balance keeping an emotional distance without being cold and uncaring? It seemed next to impossible.

At her words, Penny's smile faltered, but only for a moment. "Well, let's see if we can change that, shall we?"

Halfway through browsing the racks of elegant vintage clothing, Kat forgot all about her reticence. Penny found several items that fit her like a glove—including a pair of caramel-colored driving gloves in the softest suede imaginable.

While boisterous Christmas music played in the background, she tried on various ensembles, posing in front of a large gilded mirror. Penny even brought over a plate of sugar cookies and scrumptious tea, nibbling on the refreshments while she added snippets of commentary on each outfit as though they were in a movie montage.

In the merriment, all of Kat's self-conscious reservations slipped away, and she hardly recognized her cheerful, glowing complexion reflected back at her.

How was it possible that she'd barely met this woman and already felt as though they'd known each other their entire lives?

And how could she keep their unexpected bond from growing any stronger?

Before someone got hurt.

❄

*K*eeping one eye on the front door, Jack scrubbed the wraparound bar for the hundredth time. If he wasn't careful, he'd rub the shellac right off and wouldn't be able to slide the old-fashioned soda glasses across the counter with the same level of ease.

Every time the door hinges creaked, his heart catapulted into his throat. And every time someone entered the diner who wasn't Kat, it plummeted into his stomach.

Even in the midst of stalking the entrance, he found his level of interest baffling. It wasn't as if he had feelings for the woman. He'd known her for a grand total of ten seconds. But the truth was, no one had affected him as strongly since his ex.

Ashley Tanner had flipped his world upside down the moment she'd walked into it in sixth grade. More like *sashayed* into it. She'd possessed a level of confidence most girls her age couldn't even fathom. And yet, she wasn't arrogant or condescending. Her kindness had attracted him as much as her ink-black eyes and full lips perpetually poised on the edge of a smile. Completely captivated by her charm, he would have done anything for her—except abandon Poppy Creek and all of his principles.

The door burst open, letting in a rush of cold air, and Jack's gaze once again darted toward the latest arrival.

Disappointment mixed with dread as Mayor Burns strode inside as though stepping out of a Wall Street board meeting. Dressed in a slick cashmere coat, Burberry scarf, and leather gloves, the man certainly wasn't subtle. In fact, in Jack's opinion, he exemplified the expression *big fish in a small pond*. It wouldn't have bothered Jack if the mayor didn't seem so determined to expand his swimming hole.

"Jack! Just the man I wanted to see." Burns plastered on a smarmy smile.

"What can I get for you today, Mayor?" The man never actually sat down to eat in Jack's establishment. Probably for fear the diner's tasteless decor would taint his designer duds. But he wasn't above ordering takeout on a regular basis.

"Nothing today. I just came by to tell you about the Christmas Carnival we're hosting this year. You weren't at the town meeting." His last sentence carried a hint of censure.

Jack suppressed a groan. He'd purposely stopped going to the meetings because he found the mayor's relentless schemes to increase tourism tiring.

But he'd heard about the latest marketing effort through the rumor mill. Burns wanted to hold a huge holiday extravaganza inviting all the neighboring towns to participate. At the end of the night, he'd grandiosely bestow an award for the best holiday display—probably as an excuse to give another one of his famously verbose speeches.

All well and good until he'd wanted to replace the long-standing tradition of Pajama Christmas—which Burns deemed trite and childish—but he'd been overruled, thankfully. Instead, he'd moved the event to Christmas Day. Or rather, the evening of Christmas Day, claiming the carnival would be the perfect way to close out the holiday.

"I've heard about it," Jack told him, trying to keep his mounting irritation from creeping into his voice.

"Wonderful! Then I don't need to tell you that I expect your display to be done as soon as possible."

"*My* display?" He'd assumed participation was optional. He didn't have time to put out a potted poinsettia let alone organize an elaborate storefront display.

Burns sighed heavily. "Jack, I shouldn't have to impress upon you the importance of town-wide cooperation. We're a community. And as such, it's important we all participate. Don't tell me you're short on Christmas spirit this year?"

Jack bristled. This wasn't the first time they'd butted heads. Burns had been pestering him for years to "revitalize" the diner, as he put it. He made it sound like Jack's restaurant was a neglected landmark in need of massive reconstruction—or demolition.

Wringing the dishrag tightly in his hands, Jack muttered, "Sure thing, Mr. Mayor."

"Excellent. I look forward to seeing your best efforts." With a smug grin, Burns turned on his heel.

Gritting his teeth, Jack resisted the urge to flick his retreating backside with the damp towel. The man had a lot of nerve spouting off about the importance of community. But what irked him the most was the mayor's jab at his lack of Christmas spirit.

As much as he hated to admit it, he *was* in short supply this year. Between the cancelation of his sister's visit, his misgivings about Kat, and now the added pressure to create a Burns-approved storefront spectacle, he'd almost run out.

CHAPTER 7

$\mathcal{A}$s they approached the restaurant, Kat's gaze immediately flew to the wooden sign above the entrance.

Jack's Diner.

Heat crept up her neck. Could it be owned by her Jack? Well, not *her* Jack. The Jack she'd met earlier. The Jack who— She shook her head sharply, abruptly halting her ridiculous train of thought.

Squaring her shoulders, she followed Penny through the heavy, solid oak door. Hundreds of men were named Jack. And even if it did turn out to be the same one, so what? He was nothing more than a kind stranger she'd met on the street.

Despite her assertion, her body temperature continued to rise, splashing color across her cheeks. She stubbornly blamed the effect on the hearty fire crackling in the stone hearth.

"This place is… rustic." Kat took in the abundance of plaid upholstery, exposed brick walls, and the rough-hewn wood beams stretched across the ceiling.

"Country charm at its finest." Penny smiled as she shrugged

out of her jacket. Draping it over her arm, she ambled toward a cozy booth in the back.

"Shouldn't we wait to be seated?" Kat glanced around for a hostess. The restaurant bustled with activity even though it couldn't be more than five o'clock.

"I always sit in the same booth, if it's available." Penny plucked the menu from between a bottle of barbecue sauce and ketchup. "Colt says I might as well carve my name on it."

"Colt?" Kat grabbed a second menu and cracked it open.

"He's one of the cooks," Penny explained, her eyes sparkling "and my fiancé."

Kat's gaze fell to the antique ruby ring adorning Penny's left hand. Why hadn't she noticed it before? "Congratulations."

"Thank you! He proposed this summer while we were in Greece."

"How romantic." Kat peered closer at the ring, noticing the way the ruby sat unusually high on the intricate yellow gold setting. "I've never seen a ring like that before."

"It's called a locket ring. Or a poison ring, in some circles," she said with a wry grin. "There's a hidden compartment beneath the bezel." She gently flipped it open.

Kat leaned forward, squinting to get a closer look. "What's inside?"

"Grains of sand. The bright white flecks are from the beach in Greece where Colt proposed. The tan-colored ones are from a secluded cove you actually know quite well."

"Really?"

"They're from the beach in front of your house. Of course, I didn't know you lived there at the time. Colt brought me on a surprise date." Her features softened. "Truthfully, it was the best date of my life. We had a romantic picnic, built a sandcastle together, and watched the bioluminescent waves crash against the shore. Then, before we left, he gathered some sand in a tiny jar as a memento."

Kat listened in amazement. "That was *you?*" she cried, recalling how Fern had asked for her help to arrange everything on the beach. Since Starcross Cove had a reputation for reuniting star-crossed couples, it wasn't uncommon to assist romantic souls who believed in the legend. But to think… on that occasion it had been her own sister!

"Small world, isn't it?"

"Sure is," Kat murmured, suddenly parched.

Thankfully, a man approached their table with two glasses of iced water. "Hey, Penny. I'll let Colt know you're here." His gravelly voice matched his rough-around-the-edges appearance, yet his broad, genuine smile created an appealing contrast.

"Thanks, Vick."

When he was out of earshot, Penny asked, "What about you? Anyone special in your life?"

Kat nearly choked on an ice cube, sputtering as she lowered her glass. Plucking a paper towel from the roll that served as a substitute for standard table linens, she dabbed the moisture from her chin. "Dating isn't really on my to-do list."

"Any particular reason?"

"Let's just say I didn't have the best role model." Kat's gaze fell to her hands where the paper towel lay crumpled in her tightly clenched fist.

"You don't like talking about her, do you?"

Even though their mother's name never left her lips, Kat knew exactly who Penny meant, as if Helena Bennet would forever be an unspoken bond between them. "No, not really."

"Well, don't worry. I promise I won't pry you with a million questions. As far as I'm concerned, we never have to mention her again."

Kat's head jerked up in surprise.

"This might seem a little strange," Penny said softly, "but growing up, my dad used to tell me all these fantastical stories about Helena. He made her sound like a magical creature in a fairy tale, and I got used to thinking of her in that way—like she wasn't real. Looking back, I think my dad thought it would be easier than telling me the truth, that she simply didn't love us anymore."

At the look of quiet resignation on Penny's face, Kat's heart ached. And yet, she also felt a tiny pang of envy. There had been countless times she'd tried to trick herself into believing parts of her childhood were merely a bad dream, but it had never worked.

"Of course, that being said," Penny added with an air of irony, "Helena was the reason I didn't date for a long time. I couldn't imagine falling in love after witnessing how badly she'd broken my father's heart."

Kat stared at the mangled wad of paper in her palm as guilt and remorse swelled in her chest. She hated the thought that others had suffered at her mother's hand. But she couldn't escape the reality that Helena Bennet had left behind misfortune like fingerprints, marring everything she touched.

"What changed?" The question escaped before she could stop it, and Kat immediately regretted prolonging the conversation. It teetered too close to unwanted territory.

"Everything," Penny said simply. As she was about to expound, a man with dark blond hair and a dimpled grin slipped into the booth beside her. Kissing her cheek, he draped his arm around her shoulders in an easy, familiar gesture.

A sweet, self-conscious blush dusted Penny's cheeks as a loving glance passed between them.

Kat ignored the hollow feeling in the pit of her stomach at the knowledge she'd never experience that kind of intimacy for herself.

"I was beginning to think you'd changed your mind," the man said with an affectionate smile. "This is closer to an early dinner than a late lunch."

"I know. I'm sorry. I forgot we needed to do a little shopping first. I definitely wouldn't forget something this huge." Penny's grin broadened. "Colt, this is my sister, Kat. Kat, this is my fiancé, Colt."

Keeping one arm around Penny, Colt extended his free hand. "Nice to meet you."

"Nice to meet you, too." Kat noticed his grip was both friendly and firm—a fact she appreciated. She hated when men assumed they would crush her delicate bones if they gave her a proper handshake.

"Is Jack in the kitchen?" Penny asked. "I'd like him to meet Kat, too."

Kat's pulse stuttered to a stop, and she quickly blurted, "Oh, I don't want to bother him. I'm sure he's busy."

"He can spare a few minutes," Colt assured her. "In fact, there he is now. Hey, Jack! C'mon over here and meet Kat."

It took all of Kat's resolve not to slink beneath the table.

*S*uppressing a groan, Jack momentarily ignored Colt's clamoring as he handed Dolores Whittaker her takeout container of fragrant garlic and rosemary chicken. He should've known the second he left the kitchen he'd be asking for trouble.

The elderly woman's blue eyes twinkled behind her Coke-bottle glasses as she said, "I think Colt wants you to meet that beautiful young lady seated with him and Penny. You shouldn't keep her waiting."

"Yes, ma'am," he said dutifully. Even though he'd graduated from high school years ago, he still saw her as the principal's wife. "You be careful carrying that to your car." He nodded toward the brown paper bag. "I added some extra potatoes with the parsley and shallots you like so much, so the container is a little heavy."

"You're a dear."

Jack watched her shuffle out the front door, taking a moment to gather his nerve before answering his summons.

As he neared the table, his stomach twisted into uncomfortable knots. Somehow, Kat managed to look even more beautiful than before, and he couldn't help noticing her rosy glow, almost as if she felt as self-conscious as he did.

"Hey, there." He mustered a welcoming smile despite his sudden lack of oxygen. "Is this man bothering you? I keep telling him he's supposed to take the customer's order not canoodle with them."

"I think he's trying to guarantee a good tip," Penny teased. "Jack, this is my sister, Kat. Kat, this is our good friend, Jack. He owns the diner."

"Actually, we've already met," he admitted, trying not to recall the brazen way he'd asked her out—or her polite rejection.

"You have?" Penny asked, sounding surprised.

"Earlier today. She attacked me on the sidewalk in front of your store." As he met Kat's gaze, he tried to keep a straight face, unable to resist teasing her.

"Hey!" she protested, her tone matching his mirth. "It was self-defense. You could have been a mugger."

"True." He nodded in mock seriousness. "Poppy Creek is well known for its shocking crime rate."

Her lips twitched as though holding back a laugh.

"Interesting…" Colt glanced between them, both eyebrows raised.

Catching his friend's scheming expression, Jack cleared his throat. "So, what would you two ladies like to order this evening?"

"I'll have the cinnamon-and-coffee steak with a side of grilled asparagus and roasted potatoes, please." Penny closed her menu and propped it between the condiment bottles.

"And I'd love the mother lode chili and cornbread," Kat added, nestling her menu beside Penny's.

For a moment, Jack simply stared. Based on Colt's gossip from earlier, he'd expected her to choose one of the fancier options, which wasn't fair considering he barely knew her. A tiny pang of guilt—and embarrassment—pricked his heart for judging her so quickly.

"Excellent choice," he said warmly. "One of my favorites."

"Hey, I just had an idea," Colt cut in. "Penny and I have a date night planned for this evening, but why don't the four of us do something together? We can give Kat a tour of Poppy Creek before she heads home."

Jack straightened, immediately sobered by Colt's words. *Before she heads home...* He'd do well to remember her presence in town was only temporary.

"That's very kind of you," Kat said with a strained smile. "But I'm pretty worn out from the long drive today. If you don't mind, I think I'll call it a night once we finish dinner."

While Colt and Penny expressed how they understood, but would miss her, Jack couldn't have been more relieved.

The only way he could positively avoid *not* falling for this woman was to stay as far away from her as possible.

CHAPTER 8

*C*s the car tires rattled down the gravel road, Kat gripped the steering wheel in silent frustration. Although they'd labored over the riddle during dinner—even asking Colt for help —they weren't able to reach a satisfying conclusion. In desperation, they'd settled on two flimsy possibilities—Timothy's telescope and the sundial—based on the riddle's references to the sun and stars. But neither option seemed to encompass the entire riddle, and Kat wasn't surprised when they checked both locations after dinner and came up empty-handed.

At this rate, she'd be stuck in Poppy Creek forever.

Passing through an open gate, she sucked in a breath as a stunning Victorian home came into view, its buttery yellow exterior illuminated by twinkling Christmas lights in a soft, golden hue.

After parking in the covered carport, Kat climbed out of the driver's seat only to stand perfectly still, in awe of her surroundings. Lush green vines ambled up each side of the stately exterior as if swaddling the residence in a warm blanket. Based on the inn's name, Kat wondered if they were morning glory vines and imagined how the building would look engulfed in vibrant indigo flowers in the springtime.

But her favorite feature was the inviting front porch that boasted a cozy seating area generous enough to accommodate several guests. Lanterns flickered on the tabletops and thick throw blankets were draped over the plush couches and chairs.

As she gazed at the idyllic setting, a familiar longing filled her heart. In the quiet moments, when she allowed herself to dream, she'd envision running an inn of her own, even grander than this one, with enough space to host workshops like pottery, quilting, and stained-glass. Maybe even self-defense classes, if she so chose. Possibly even large enough for its own elegant restaurant.

But above all, she dreamed of keeping the most opulent suite available for someone in need of a rejuvenating retreat but who couldn't afford it. Someone like Fern or one of their many Hope Hideaway residents.

Of course, that's all it was—a silly dream. She'd never leave Fern or Starcross Cove. And yet, she found herself drawn to discovering what else the Morning Glory Inn had to offer, to tuck away the inspiration for future quiet moments.

Lugging the shopping bags of clothing from Penny's store up the broad porch steps, she couldn't help noticing every thoughtful detail, from the basket of lawn games to the rack of fishing poles. The owners of the establishment certainly seemed keen on ensuring their guests had a good time during their stay.

Kat breathed a contented sigh as a delicate bell chimed, greeting her as she crossed the threshold. Immediately, the homey scent of gingerbread enveloped her like a welcoming hug.

"Hello, dearie! Welcome to the Morning Glory Inn. You must be Kat." Seemingly from out of nowhere, a lithe, sprightly woman appeared in the hallway. "I'm Gertrude Hobbs, but everyone calls me Trudy. Here, let me help you with those." Without waiting for a response—or a hello—Trudy plucked the bags from Kat's grasp, unconcerned with the fact that both of her hands—and every inch of her festive apron—were covered in flour.

Flitting toward the antique check-in desk, Trudy called out over her shoulder, "It's a Christmas miracle I had a room available. Not more than two minutes before Penny called, a guest canceled. Her mother took ill, the poor dear. Nothing too serious, thank goodness. But she didn't feel right leaving her home alone under the circumstances, which is perfectly understandable. At my age, the sniffles can turn to pneumonia quicker than the time it takes to boil a pot of chicken soup."

Kat hid a smile as Trudy set the bags on the polished hardwood floor before flipping open her guestbook. The woman sure had the gift of gab.

"That's why my husband, George, and I have a full refund cancellation policy," she continued. "Things happen outside our control. And the last thing the poor dear needs is financial stress on top of an ill mother. Besides, our rooms rarely stay empty for long. As the only inn in Poppy Creek, our No Vacancy sign is practically a permanent fixture."

"You're the only lodging in Poppy Creek?" Kat asked, speaking for the first time since her arrival.

"Officially, yes. And let me tell you, it can put quite the strain on two old-timers who've been running this place for nearly forty years. Although, Dolores Whittaker has been known to put up a guest or two in her large farmhouse. She lives by herself, you know. And I think she likes the company. Would you believe she does it all online? It's amazing what you can do with technology these days. But I prefer to handle everything the old-fashioned way."

She plucked a brass key from a wall of hooks behind her, passing it to Kat by the end of a green satin ribbon. "You'll be staying in the Cedar Suite upstairs. It doesn't face the garden, but you have a prime view of the forest, which looks lovely covered in snow. And we're supposed to get a nice storm sometime this weekend. Not according to the weather station, of course. But Bill Tucker's pig, Peggy Sue, has been accurately predicting snowstorms for years."

"Unfortunately, I'll only be staying one night." For a fleeting moment, Kat regretted her brief visit. Since she'd lived her whole life on the coast of California, she'd never seen snow before.

"Oh, now that's a shame." Trudy made a *tsk-tsk* sound in tandem with a disappointed shake of her head. "Well, I'll hold off on booking your room for the rest of the week in case you change your mind. Christmas in Poppy Creek is a magical time of year. You really can't appreciate it unless you stay a few days, at least."

Before Kat could respond, a loud *trill* reverberated down the hallway.

Trudy clapped her hands, scattering a puff of flour. "Oh, heavens! I forgot all about the cookies." Scampering from behind the desk, she said, "I'll have George carry your bags up to your room. I'd love to stay and chat, but time waits for no man, as the saying goes."

Something about the woman's words resonated with Kat, but she wasn't sure why. "I can carry my own bags, but thanks for the offer. You take care of those cookies."

"Thank you, dear. Do come down once you're settled in. We're watching *White Christmas* tonight and we'd love for you to join us." With a fluttering wave, Trudy scuttled down the hallway and disappeared from sight.

Lifting her bags off the floor, Kat smiled. Trudy was an interesting woman, to say the least, but Kat appreciated her warm, gregarious demeanor.

As she mounted the creaking staircase, admiring the eclectic assortment of artwork hanging on the wall, Trudy's words echoed inside her head.

Time waits for no man….

Why did the phrase sound so familiar?

Juggling her belongings, she eased open the door to her suite. Her breath immediately caught in her throat. Directly across from the threshold, a fully decorated Christmas tree sparkled in front of an expansive bay window, its silvery lights glittering around the room like tiny prisms. The fragrant branches dispersed the most delightful aroma of fresh cedar, and Kat briefly closed her eyes, savoring the scent.

As her eyelids drifted open, she noticed two snug reading chairs arranged in front of a quaint potbelly stove. A queen-size canopy bed rested against the opposite wall, its thick quilt dotted with embroidered evergreen trees.

She set the shopping bags on the tufted bench at the foot of the bed before crossing the room to inspect an exquisite grandfather clock similar to one she'd seen in Penny's apartment. Rather than numbers on the dial, the hands ticked past images depicting the various phases of the moon and sun.

As she studied the unusual design, Trudy's words flooded her mind.

Time waits for no man.

Retrieving her cell phone from her coat pocket, Kat pulled up the photo she'd taken of the riddle.

The stars wait for no man.

That's why it sounded so familiar! Her pulse quickened as the pieces started to fall into place.

The stars wait for no man, and neither does the sun. Once you think it's over, it's really just begun.

Each line could be referring to the passage of time. Which meant...

She hastily scrolled through her contacts, looking for the number Penny had programmed into her phone earlier, then remembered her date with Colt—the one her fiancé had attempted to turn into a double date.

While sweet, the offer had been grossly misguided. Not only

did being around Penny elicit too many painful memories, but spending time with Jack evoked an emotion far worse... *hope*.

*G*rateful for his one remaining single friend, Jack welcomed Reed Hollis into his home with a boisterous grin, which broadened when he caught sight of the white paper bag in his hand. The Sadie's Sweet Shop logo stamped on the front instantly made his mouth water and he snatched it from Reed's grasp.

"What'd you bring?" The paper crinkled as Jack rooted around inside.

"All your favorites, don't worry." Reed shrugged out of his sherpa-lined coat, hanging it on a rustic hook by the front door. "I wasn't sure if Grant would be home, so I brought enough for three of us."

Jack shoved a pecan caramel square into his mouth, amused by Reed's comment. Although Grant lived in the cozy guesthouse behind his cabin—which he'd originally built for his sister's visits —he rarely saw him anymore. Ever since he got engaged, Grant spent most of his time with Eliza, Ben, and their dog, Vinny, basically using the guesthouse as a place to sleep. "It's just you and me tonight. Two sad bachelors stuffing their faces with chocolate."

"Hey," Reed laughed, kicking his boots off before flopping onto the couch. "I brought taffy and licorice, too."

A sucker for the sweet, star anise flavor, Jack dug inside the bag, finally retrieving a handful of black licorice shaped like lumps of coal—fitting, given his grinch status this year. Satisfied with his selection for the moment, he handed the bag back to Reed before sinking into his oversize plaid recliner.

"I was surprised you called," Reed admitted, choosing an amaretto truffle for himself. "Doesn't Lucy usually visit this time of year?"

The slippery candy slid down Jack's throat, lodging in his esophagus. Coughing violently, he pounded a fist against his chest until it shook loose, reopening his airways.

"Are you okay?" Reed asked with concern.

"I'm fine," Jack croaked, his eyes watering. Leaping to his feet, he crossed the short distance to the kitchen and poured himself a glass of water. When he'd finally caught his breath, he shared, "Lucy can't make it this year."

"Oh, man. I'm sorry. I know how much you look forward to seeing her."

"Thanks. I'll miss her, but life happens." Rather, his *parents* happened, but he didn't feel like going into the dreary details at the moment.

While Reed arranged the deck of cards on the coffee table for their game of gin rummy, Jack set a saucepan on the stove to make a quick batch of apple cider, trying not to think about Lucy's canceled trip.

What he wouldn't give to have his little sister back in Poppy Creek for good. For a time, he'd even considered setting her up with Reed. In Jack's opinion, she couldn't do better than his kind and dependable friend who made a stable, honest living running his own nursery that specialized in rare varieties of roses. What girl didn't like flowers? Besides, according to the number of female tourists who swooned over his "boy-next-door" vibe and "soulful" brown eyes, he wasn't bad looking, either.

But for all Jack's not-so-subtle hints, Reed seemed to be pining after someone else, although he'd never talk about it no matter how much he pried. Not that Jack could blame him. He never talked about the day Ashley left. For all his friends knew, their breakup had been mutual. That was the unexpected side effect of being the eldest child in a large family—he got used to taking care of his siblings' problems and burying his own.

Maybe if he put a little more energy into his own life, he wouldn't be so lonely.

CHAPTER 9

"Come in, come in." Bright-eyed and breathless, Penny held the door open and waved for Kat to step inside the apartment. "I'm so glad you solved it!"

"*Maybe*. It's not too early, is it? I confess to being a little anxious to find out if my guess is correct." She'd forced herself to wait until seven and raced over, skipping Trudy's scrumptious-smelling breakfast, though the mouthwatering aroma of freshly baked banana bread had tempted her resolve as she'd rushed out the front door.

"Not at all. Honestly, I could hardly sleep. I kept going over the riddle all night. I'd almost forgotten how much I enjoyed my dad's treasure hunts."

Kat wasn't sure she'd use the word *enjoy* to describe her experience thus far, but she did feel exhilarated at the prospect of finding the brooch.

As she stood in front of the grandfather clock, her heart stopped when she noticed two keyholes on the upper and lower compartments encasing the dial and pendulum.

"Don't look so worried." Popping onto her tiptoes, Penny reached behind a decorative spire on top and retrieved a small gold key. "Dad used to keep it locked so I wouldn't play with the mechanism." After she unlocked both doors, she nodded toward the bottom one. "You check in there. I imagine he would have taped it somewhere along the inside walls."

Careful not to disrupt the brass weights and pendulum, Kat ran her hand along the inner edge, feeling for anything out of the ordinary. After several minutes of searching, she bit back an excited squeal as her fingers grazed an unusual lump.

"Did you find it?" Penny asked eagerly.

"I'm not sure." After gently peeling back the tape, Kat withdrew her hand. Her heart sank. "It's just a dusty piece of paper."

"Oh." Penny scrunched her face in disappointment. "I was afraid that might happen."

"That what might happen?"

"I think it's another clue. I didn't want to mention it earlier in case I was wrong, but the treasure hunts usually had more than one." She offered a sheepish smile.

Mildly irritated by the revelation, Kat unfolded the note and read the clue out loud. "'From death comes life, often felt but never seen. Getting too close may cause strife, but you can still enjoy the gleam.'" Meeting Penny's gaze she asked, "Any ideas?"

Penny held out her hand, and Kat passed her the note, waiting anxiously as her sister studied the peculiar phrasing. Finally, she glanced up with an apologetic grimace. "Sorry, but nothing comes to mind."

Frustrated, Kat placed both hands behind her head and filled her lungs with a deep breath as she stared at the ceiling. *Think, Kat, think... what could it mean?*

"Maybe something related to cooking or food?" Penny offered. "You know, from death—of an animal or a plant—comes life, as in sustenance?"

"Maybe. But you can see an animal or plant."

"True." Penny tapped a finger to her lips.

They stood in silence, each deep in thought, for several

minutes until Penny said brightly, "Why don't we get some breakfast? We might think better on a full stomach and I don't open the shop for another hour."

"That's a good idea." Kat slipped out her phone, wondering how she would tell Fern her secret mission had been delayed yet again, perhaps for an indeterminate amount of time. "Is there somewhere I can get a strong cup of coffee? I could use a jolt of caffeine."

"I know just the place." Penny grinned.

*A*s Kat took a languid sip of the aromatic brew, her worries melted away. The blend—aptly named Christmas Morning—had hints of cinnamon, gingerbread, and caramel. "This tastes incredible," she murmured, not wasting any time before taking another generous gulp.

"I'm so glad you like it." Cassie Davis, the café's owner, beamed. "It's a new blend. I'm playing around with adding flavored syrups to the coffee after it's been roasted. Have you met Frank yet?"

Kat shook her head, barely removing her lips from the rim of the mug.

"Oh, I do hope you get a chance to meet him while you're in town. He taught me how to roast coffee," she explained. "He's a purist through and through and claims flavored coffee is worse than decaf. But, as I frequently remind him, he's not always right. Although, he usually is." She laughed in a way that highlighted her obvious affection for the man.

"Well, I'm on your side," Kat told her. "This has just become my new favorite blend. Do you sell by the pound? I'd love to bring some home with me." Kat knew it would be an instant hit with Hope Hideaway residents and would pair perfectly with Fern's Milagros.

"Of course! I'll grab you a pound. On the house."

Before Kat could politely decline her generosity, Cassie had spun on her heel, heading toward the other side of the room where one-pound coffee bags were neatly arranged on a display shelf.

Kat looked on, completely incredulous. How did anyone make a living in this town if they always gave everything away?

"If you think the coffee is good, wait until you try the cinnamon roll." Penny tore off a soft, gooey chunk and popped it in her mouth. Her expression bordered on euphoric as she licked the cream cheese icing off of her fingertips.

A quiet yet unsettling realization stole over Kat as she savored her pastry and coffee—she could easily make a home for herself in a town like Poppy Creek. So far, she loved everything about it, especially the cozy café. Between the creative menu offering festive delights like Sugar Plum Fairy Pie and Kris Kringle Cappuccinos, and the chalkboard display listing some sort of countdown of holiday traditions, the place exuded a sense of Christmas magic she'd never experienced before. But she could certainly get used to it.

There was just one not-so-insignificant problem—every time she looked at her sister, it was as if their mother stared back at her. And with each glance, distressing memories overshadowed every ounce of joy; Helena's lingering presence affected Kat even after her death.

"Here you go." Disrupting her melancholy thoughts, Cassie set the kraft bag on table.

"Thank you so much. I'm happy to pay for it." Kat reached into her coat pocket for her wallet, but Cassie dismissed her offer.

"Don't be silly. Consider it a souvenir."

Kat was about to insist on paying for it one last time, but the bell chimed above the entrance, stealing her attention.

As Jack Gardener strolled through the front door, she instantly forgot about everything else.

❄

*J*ack could've sworn he felt her presence even before he spotted Kat at the table by the window. Sunlight glittered through the frosted glass, making her red hair sparkle.

Relax, Jack. Keep your eye on the prize.

The prize being a triple-shot chai latte with an extra dash of cardamom.

"Jack!"

He froze as Cassie called him over to the table.

"Good morning, ladies." He tried to keep his focus on Cassie as he crossed the room, but his stubborn gaze kept drifting in a different direction.

"Have you come up with an idea for your display yet?" she asked.

"Not even close. But I need to start working on it today. Which is why I'm here. I figured a little caffeine would bolster my pitiful creativity."

Turning to Kat, Penny explained, "Our mayor has asked each business owner to come up with a storefront display to make the town square extra festive for our Christmas Carnival in a few weeks."

"We do something similar in Starcross Cove."

"Really?" Penny asked. "Did you make one for Hope Hideaway?"

"The community center, actually. Our theme was Moonlight and Mistletoe. It was fairly simple—an arbor decorated with mistletoe and twinkle lights, but it looked stunning in the evening. People loved it. Especially the couples."

"What a great idea!" Cassie cried in excitement. "Jack, why

don't you do something like that for the diner? It sounds simple enough."

"Especially if you still have the arbor you took down when you expanded the back patio a few years ago," Penny added.

Jack rubbed his stubbled jaw, mulling over the idea. "I'm not sure I can picture how it's supposed to look, though. How would I go about attaching the mistletoe?" He definitely liked the sound of something simple, but it may be beyond his artistic capabilities.

"Kat," Cassie began, her eyes twinkling, "do you think you could spare a few hours to help Jack? I'm afraid he's a little hopeless when it comes to decor."

Kat's eyes widened, and she looked as surprised as he felt. "Right now?"

"If you don't mind," Cassie said sweetly. "I'm sure Jack would appreciate having the task off his to-do list."

Jack opened his mouth, but no words came out. Why did this feel like a setup?

"I have to open the shop in a few minutes, anyway," Penny added. "Maybe focusing on some other tasks for a while will refresh our brains and stimulate new ideas."

Jack had no clue what Penny was talking about, but it seemed to mean something to Kat, alleviating some of her reticence.

"Sure," she answered slowly, offering him a timid smile.

It was the first time they'd made eye contact since he'd approached their table, and his breath caught in his throat.

He tried to reciprocate, but the muscles in his face refused to cooperate and wound up twisting into a goofy, lopsided grin—not his finest moment.

How on earth would he get through the next few hours without making a total fool out of himself?

Or falling even harder for this woman than he already had.

CHAPTER 10

*A*fter they'd ensured Jack still had the arbor in storage, they headed a few miles outside of town to gather the mistletoe.

Kat still couldn't believe she'd been roped into the excursion. Although she'd enjoyed working on the display last Christmas, spending the afternoon with Jack Gardener made her uneasy. She found him much more appealing than she wanted to admit.

Not because of his charisma—she didn't trust charm. To be honest, she couldn't quite pinpoint why she felt so drawn to him. She suspected it had something to do with his kind eyes—the gateway to a person's soul, as Fern described them. They were warm and unguarded, yet she could tell he'd seen his share of pain, too. She wasn't sure if she believed in kindred spirits, but if she did, Jack Gardener would certainly come close.

As they rattled down a dirt road, she gripped the worn handle of the passenger door, cringing as every nut and bolt in the ancient Chevy pickup seemed ready to shake loose. In hindsight, she should have driven herself. At least then she wouldn't have been forced to sit in such close proximity, inhaling his heady scent of chicory and woodsmoke.

"Are we almost there?" she asked as they turned down an even more dilapidated lane.

No sooner than the question left her lips, she gasped as a breathtaking home came into view.

Or rather, a *mansion* would be more accurate. Two stories tall, the palatial Colonial-style estate boasted a grandiose front porch, stately columns, and several chimneys. There had to be dozens of rooms inside, not to mention a wing composed almost entirely of tall, elegant windows.

"What is this place?" It appeared fit for royalty except clearly no one had lived inside in decades. The white exterior paint had all but peeled away and the windows that weren't boarded were coated in dust and grime. She almost wept to see so much beauty in such horrendous disrepair.

"It's nothing special. Just a house no one lives in anymore," Jack said simply, parking at the end of the circular driveway.

"Are you serious?" Kat hopped out of the truck, her eyes wide and incredulous. "It's the most stunning home I've ever seen. Why would anyone leave it like this?"

Jack shrugged, striding toward the bed of the truck to unload their supplies.

Kat surveyed the neglected structure, her chest swelling with emotion. What a gut-wrenching waste! Whoever owned this property should be ashamed of themselves. Didn't they realize some people would give anything to own a building this beautiful?

"Ready?" Jack asked, arranging a ladder between a pair of slender tree trunks.

For the first time since their arrival, Kat pried her gaze from the mournful mansion and noticed it was surrounded by towering sycamores. Though they'd lost most of their leaves, they still looked regal, their blanched bark dazzling in the afternoon sunlight. Glancing up, she noticed large bundles of mistletoe draped in their spindly branches.

"I'll chop them down, you catch them in this."

Their fingers grazed as he handed her a five-gallon bucket, and he made no effort to release his grip. Her breath hitched as he tilted his chin, gazing up at the mistletoe above their heads. "You know…" he drawled, his eyes glinting.

Flustered, she yanked the bucket from his grasp and blurted, "Don't worry, this is strictly professional. I promise, I won't kiss you under the mistletoe."

The humor immediately left his eyes and he cleared his throat. "Glad to hear it. Otherwise, with this amount of mistletoe, we'd never get any work done." He grinned, but it lacked its usual warmth and sincerity.

She returned his smile, equally forced. What was wrong with her? Why did she say that? Ugh. She wished she could take it back.

"We should hurry," he said crisply. "The temperature just dropped."

As they worked in silence, Kat mentally berated herself for her slipup, then agonized over why it bothered her so much. It wasn't as if she *wanted* to kiss Jack under the mistletoe.

Because she most certainly didn't.

❄

*J*ack hacked into the clump of mistletoe a little more vigorously than necessary. He needed to get a grip.

So what if she promised not to kiss him under the mistletoe? It wasn't as if he'd expected her to. They barely knew each other. But for some reason, realizing the possibility was now off the table made his heart sink to the pit of his stomach.

To add another blow to the afternoon, he hadn't anticipated her strong reaction to seeing the house. The property—and all of its untenable implications—left such a bitter taste in his mouth, he often forgot other people found it attractive. Kat had been so taken with it, she seemed to think the hands-off owner had committed some sort of travesty.

So much for a perfect outing together. In fact, Jack couldn't imagine things going any worse.

Just then, a single snowflake settled on the end of his nose.

Warily, he glanced up, his gut clenching as he took in the canopy of dense storm clouds overhead.

"Is that—" Kat gasped, drawing his attention to where she stood at the base of the ladder.

Her eyes wide with awe, she watched as delicate flecks of snow swirled around her. "It's snowing!" Stretching out her hands, she spun like a small child, her face radiating pure joy and wonder.

"You must really like the snow." Jack smiled, transfixed by how beautiful she looked, her vibrant red hair sparkling with silvery specks, her cheeks flushed from the cold and excitement.

"More than I ever imagined! It's gorgeous!" She opened her mouth, catching a flake on the tip of her tongue. "It tastes good, too."

Jack chuckled as he descended the ladder. "You've never seen snow before?"

"Nope! And I don't want it to ever end!"

"Well, good news for you. It won't be stopping anytime soon. But the bad news is the flakes are getting thicker and falling faster. We need to get back into town before we're stuck here."

"If we must," she sighed, taking one last longing glance at the house. Suddenly, her eyes widened. "What's that?" She pointed toward the front porch.

Jack followed her outstretched hand, squinting at something white and lumpy protruding from behind a wide column. "I'm not sure." It was hard to see anything through the thick veil of snow.

"I think it's a dog." Before he could stop her, Kat inched

toward the house, careful not to startle the pup with sudden movements.

Jack followed close behind in case the animal proved unfriendly. As they neared the broad steps, the indistinguishable shape came into focus. Large and solid white, the dog appeared to be part Siberian husky, maybe even wolf.

"Hey there, boy," Kat purred, tiptoeing closer.

The dog's chin rested on both paws, his piercing blue eyes vacant and glassy. He didn't budge a single centimeter as they approached, his limp tail tucked beneath him.

Lowering herself an inch at a time, Kat perched on the top step and slowly extended her hand.

Jack's heart thundered inside his chest, every nerve in his body ready to leap into action if the dog lunged toward her.

But the poor weary pup barely even blinked.

Kat let the dog sniff her fingers before gently scratching the top of his head. "What a good boy," she cooed, then glanced over her shoulder. "We can't leave him here. He'll freeze."

Jack had been thinking the same thing. Without a word, he mounted the steps and crouched beside the dog. "Bear with me, buddy," he murmured, scooping his listless body into his arms. With smooth, even strides, he carried him toward the truck and nodded at the passenger door. "Would you mind?"

Kat swiftly yanked it open and stepped aside while Jack laid the dog in the center of the bench seat.

"Where are we taking him?" Kat asked, sidling onto the torn upholstery.

To Jack's surprise, the pup gingerly lifted its head and rested it on her lap. His heart melted at the sight. "How do you know it's a him?"

"I'm not sure how I can tell, but he's definitely a *him*."

He smiled at her strong conviction, then glanced at the sky, alarmed by how quickly the storm had progressed. "My house is closest. We won't have time to make it all the way back into town before the roads close."

He waited for her to argue, but she merely nodded, stroking the dog's head. Compassion seemed to flow out of her fingertips, guiding her every movement.

And while his feelings for Kat may have been pure infatuation before, something inside of him shifted in that moment.

But he didn't have time to dwell on it now.

Not if he wanted to get them home safely.

CHAPTER 11

*F*or the second time that afternoon, Kat found herself awestruck as they approached Jack's home. Poised on the edge of a picturesque lake with towering snowcapped mountains in the distance, the cozy cabin looked like a wintry paradise.

"You live here?" she asked, still dumbfounded. Although it was covered in several inches of snow, she recognized the outline of a boat secured to a short dock and a ring of Adirondack chairs by the water's edge.

"Yep. It's not much, but it's home." He parked in a rudimentary garage that appeared sturdy but austere. Stacks of firewood lined two of the three walls. The third housed a bicycle with all-terrain tires, fishing poles and tackle, and a couple of kayaks.

Kat followed close behind Jack as he carried the dog toward the house. Although it took less than a minute to span the short distance to the porch, snowflakes caked her hair and clothing.

He nodded toward the front door, which he apparently kept unlocked, and Kat nudged it open, closing it behind them to block out the storm.

As she stood in the entrance, the intimacy of invading Jack's personal space struck her all at once, leaving her nervous and uncertain.

"Can you grab a blanket and lay it in front of the fireplace?"

She followed his gaze toward a well-worn steamer trunk and popped it open. A stack of thick blankets—mostly plaid—greeted her, and she chose the fluffiest one, laying it on the hardwood floor in front of a rotund potbelly stove. Although chilly inside the cabin, warmth radiated from the black iron chamber. She suspected hot embers lingered inside from a previous fire.

Jack gently laid the pup on the makeshift bed before stoking the fire with a fresh log. It crackled and sparked as he prodded the coals, igniting a hearty blaze. "You can hang your coat by the front door. The cabin will be warm in a few minutes. The perks of living in a small space." He smiled, calling her attention to the cabin's modest size.

The kitchen, dinette, and living area could easily fit inside the formal sitting room at Hope Hideaway, but it was cozy.

Her heart raced as she draped her coat over a rustic hook before removing her damp shoes. They'd be trapped inside for hours, maybe even all night. Suddenly, her temperature rose and it had nothing to do with the roaring fire. She cleared her throat. "We should see if we can get him to eat something. Do you have broth?"

"There's a mason jar in the fridge." Jack rose and removed his coat and boots. "Are you hungry? If you want to warm the broth, I can whip up something for us."

"That would be wonderful. Thanks."

They silently worked side by side in the confined kitchen, listening to the sound of falling snow. Kat never realized it even made a sound, but she'd describe it as a faint whooshing or a soft whisper of wind. Either way, it was heavenly.

Within minutes, the mouthwatering aroma of rosemary and thyme filled the cabin as Jack threw together some chicken soup.

Kat set a bowl of broth on the floor for the pup, ecstatic when he lapped up every last drop before curling into a ball and drifting off to sleep.

"I think he's going to be just fine, thanks to you." The admiration in Jack's voice warmed her from the inside out, and she wanted to bask in the glow.

"And you," she added, her voice a bit breathy. Although she'd been attracted to Jack since the moment they met, something about rescuing the dog together drew her to him even more than before—dangerously close.

"Make yourself comfortable on the couch," he told her, ladling the soup into two enormous stoneware mugs.

She nestled into the far corner, snuggling beneath a plush blanket.

Jack handed her the steaming mug and a spoon before sitting beside her.

The couch more accurately resembled a loveseat, forcing them a little closer than Kat's comfort level. Painfully aware of his nearness, she tried to focus on the soup, savoring the creamy broth and cornucopia of pleasant spices.

"I'll ask around in the morning and see if anyone knows who the dog belongs to." Jack propped his feet on the coffee table, and Kat hid a smile, noticing the hole in his wool sock. She almost offered to darn it for him, but stopped herself in time. Darning the man's sock would definitely cross a line she needed to avoid at all costs.

Falling for Jack Gardener wasn't an option.

A fact she needed to remember now more than ever.

*N*ormally, Jack would find the falling snow and gentle crackling of the fire soothing. But sitting this close to Kat set all of his nerves on edge. She smelled like cinnamon and a hint of something sweet, and he found the combination way too alluring for his own good.

To distract himself, he proposed putting together a puzzle to pass the time. Otherwise, all he could think about was what it would be like to kiss her. And those thoughts were off-limits. Especially since Grant had texted that he, Eliza, and Ben had gotten snowed in at his parents' house, which meant Jack would be alone with Kat all night.

But in hindsight, the puzzle was a terrible idea. For some reason, all the pieces he needed were located on the other side of the coffee table, forcing him to repeatedly reach across Kat from his position on the floor, and inhale her scent.

He stared at the last piece needed to complete his corner, hoping to move it by telepathy. Finally, when it didn't budge, he gave in to the old-fashioned method.

As he reached past her, a soft curl grazed his cheek, sending his pulse into overdrive. Could she hear his sharp intake of breath? Snatching the puzzle piece, he rocked back on his heels, praying the loud thundering of his heartbeat wasn't audible.

"I'm not usually a puzzle person," Kat admitted, snapping two pieces in place with a satisfied smile. "But in the last few days, I'm becoming an expert."

"What do you mean?"

"Remember how I told you I came to Poppy Creek hoping to find something at Thistle & Thorn?"

"Yeah…."

"I was looking for a brooch that belonged to my mother. And oddly enough, Penny's dad used it as the end reward for an elaborate treasure hunt, complete with clues."

"What kind of clues?"

"Riddles. Pretty hard ones, actually. I was able to solve the first one, but now I'm stumped."

"I love riddles. Maybe I can help?"

"The more eyes on it, the better." Kat untangled her legs from her crisscross position and stood, grazing his back with her leg as she brushed past him to grab her phone from her coat pocket.

Jack had never minded the shortage of space inside his cabin before, but now he regretted not living in a palace, if only to keep from torturing himself with their close proximity.

When she returned, they bumped knees as she sat cross-legged again.

Jack bit back a groan. At this rate, he seriously doubted he'd survive the night.

"Ready?" she asked, and Jack had to remind himself that she was talking about the riddle.

"Ready."

"'From death comes life, often felt but never seen. Getting too close may cause strife, but you can still enjoy the gleam.'" She glanced up from her phone. "Any idea what it means?"

Jack pondered it a moment. "I think it's talking about a fire, maybe a fireplace."

Her brow furrowed in thought, and Jack explained his logic. "From death comes life—a tree has to die to provide firewood. And fire provides lifesaving warmth. You can see a flame, but you can't actually see the warmth, you just feel it. If you touch the flame, you'll get burned, but you can still enjoy the light it produces."

"Jack, I'm impressed. You just solved it in two seconds flat."

Flustered by her praise, he shrugged. "I don't have central heating, so I spend a lot of time building fires."

"Smart *and* humble." She flashed him a teasing smile that made his heart melt and hurt at the same time. "I owe you big-time. What do you want as a reward for solving it?"

His gaze fell to her lips and his lungs suddenly forgot how to function.

Thankfully, she didn't seem to notice. "Why don't I make you some of Fern's famous hot chocolate? It's a special family recipe."

"That sounds great," he rasped, cringing at how embarrassingly husky his voice sounded. He really needed to get ahold of himself. "Who's Fern?"

She paused halfway to the kitchen, a strange expression stealing over her, but she quickly dismissed it, saying casually, "She's the woman who raised me." Before Jack could press further, she added, "I'll need a bar of dark chocolate, whole milk, vanilla bean or extract, agave nectar or sugar, ancho powder or cayenne pepper. Oh, and cinnamon. And I don't suppose you have a *molinillo?*"

"A what?"

Kat grinned. "It's a wooden tool used to froth the milk, and it helps the chocolate dissolve. But a hand blender will do in a pinch."

As Jack assembled the ingredients—grateful he kept his own kitchen nearly as well stocked as the diner—he waited for an opportunity to ask more about Kat's childhood.

Truthfully, he wanted to learn everything he could about this woman who had undeniably captured his interest.

And maybe a little bit of his heart, too.

CHAPTER 12

*A*s Kat slowly stirred the hot chocolate on the stove, she chided herself for mentioning Fern. She'd heard the interest in Jack's voice when he'd asked about her, and Kat wanted to avoid any further discussion of her unconventional upbringing. The last thing she wanted was pity—especially from Jack.

She poured the thick, velvety liquid into two tin mugs, pleased with the sweet, spicy aroma curling from the brims. The first time Fern taught her the family recipe, she'd been twelve years old. Fern had caught her nestled in a corner of the couch on Christmas Eve, the clock creeping closer to midnight. But she wasn't waiting for Santa Claus to slide down the chimney. Her mother had slipped out of the shelter after dinner, as she often did, and hadn't returned.

Helena often disappeared for days on end, leaving Kat in Fern's care without any indication as to when she'd be back. But that year, she'd promised her daughter a *real* Christmas, and Kat had foolishly believed her.

Fern had stayed up with Kat most of the night, sipping hot chocolate and nibbling on cookies while they watched one classic

Christmas Claymation film after the next. They never spoke of Helena, who eventually arrived by noon the next day and immediately passed out in their bedroom upstairs.

As an adult, Kat often wondered why Fern kept letting them come back to the shelter. They'd been in and out so many times, she should have realized her mother was a hopeless cause. But ever the optimist, Fern didn't like giving up on anyone. And in thirty years, she'd only failed to help one woman turn her life around.

It pained Kat deeply that the one woman had been her mother. After all, even Ebenezer Scrooge had found redemption. Why couldn't Helena Bennet?

After handing Jack a mug of hot chocolate, she settled on the couch beside him. Their canine companion snored softly, harmonizing with the soothing crackle of the fire. "What should we call him?" she asked, watching his furry ears twitch as though he were dreaming.

"How about Fitzwilliam Darcy? But we can call him Fitz for short."

Kat blinked in surprise. "You're a Jane Austen fan?"

"Does that shock you?" he chuckled.

"Frankly, yes."

"How prejudiced of you, Miss Bennet," he said with a playful grin.

Kat laughed. "Point taken. But you have to admit, it's unusual. Most men don't read Jane Austen voluntarily."

"My sister left behind a copy of *Pride and Prejudice* after one of her visits, and on a whim, I gave it a try. Scout's honor, I enjoyed it."

Kat cocked her head, completely taken by this new information. Could the man be any more endearing?

"So, what do you think of the name?" he prompted.

"I think it suits him perfectly. Does this mean you'll keep him if we can't find his owner?" she asked hopefully.

"Maybe."

Her heart sank at his noncommittal tone, and she wasn't sure why it was suddenly so important to her that Jack kept him. After all, as long as Fitz went to a good home, it shouldn't matter. It wasn't as if she'd be around to visit.

With his brow furrowed deep in thought, Jack brought the mug to his lips.

Kat watched him intently, gauging his reaction.

After he took his first sip, his eyes widened. "Uh-oh."

"What's wrong?" She leaned forward, her pulse quickening. Did he hate it? Not everyone appreciated the subtle kick of cayenne and cinnamon.

"We have a problem," he said, his eyes glinting with humor. "This is the best hot chocolate I've ever tasted."

She relaxed against the cushions, and the corner of her mouth quirked. "And that's a problem?"

"It sure is." He took another languid sip before explaining, "Sadie Hamilton is famous around here for her hot chocolate. I can't tell her I prefer someone else's."

"Your secret is safe with me." Her stomach fluttered, pleased by his response.

"You said a woman named Fern taught you how to make it?" he asked, disrupting her moment of contentment.

"Mm-hmm…" she mumbled evasively, burying her face in the mug of hot chocolate, nearly scorching the tip of her nose.

"You said she raised you?" he continued with a soft, tactful tone. "Were you adopted?"

She squirmed, wishing they could work on the puzzle in companionable silence instead. "No, not officially."

To her relief, he didn't press further. But he regarded her closely as he took another sip of the rich, sultry drink.

Kat shifted beneath his gaze, conflicted by the warmth and kindness reflected in the deep pools of blue. Suddenly, every instinct to avoid intimacy at all costs slipped away like a fragile wisp of steam. "My mom wasn't around much during my child-hood. We didn't have what you'd call a *stable living situation.*"

His features softened as he rested the mug on his knee, giving her his full attention.

Kat stared into her own cup, too self-conscious to look anywhere else. "We were in and out of a women's shelter most of my life. And eventually, Hope Hideaway became my home. And Fern, the caretaker, became more like a mother to me than my own."

"I'm so sorry. That must have been rough."

She shrugged, touched and a little flustered by the compassion in his voice. "There are people who've experienced far worse. I was lucky to have Fern. Without her, I don't know where I'd be."

"You still keep in touch?"

"I live and work at the shelter now. My mom—" Kat hesitated. She hadn't even shared this much with Penny. Perhaps she shouldn't go any further. But then, she'd come this far. And somehow, opening up to Jack seemed to lift a heavy weight from her shoulders. She sucked in a deep breath, releasing it slowly before continuing. "My mother passed away my senior year. Fern took me in and made sure I graduated high school. Then, she offered me a job with room and board." Her voice cracked and she quickly cleared her throat.

Without saying a word, Jack laid a hand on top of hers, squeezing gently. His rough calluses felt oddly reassuring, and she didn't pull away.

"Fern sounds like an incredible woman," he said kindly.

"She is." Overcome with emotion, Kat felt her lower lip start to tremble.

Whatever you do, don't cry.

Blinking against the stinging sensation at the backs of her eyes, she tried to think of something else—anything to deter the burgeoning tears.

"And she makes the best hot chocolate," Jack added, coming to her rescue.

Grateful for the welcome levity, Kat smiled.

Somehow, he'd known exactly what she needed.

And in that moment, Kat was startled to realize what she needed... was Jack.

*L*istening to Kat's story made Jack's chest tighten, and the sudden, intense urge to protect her from pain surprised him.

Rattled, he abruptly rose and reached for her mug. "Refill?"

"That would be wonderful. Thank you."

As he strode to the kitchen, Jack grappled with his emotions, which felt too strong for his own good.

Standing at the stove, he gazed out the window, watching the snow cascade from the sky, coating the world in a blanket of white. The setting should have been peaceful. They'd notified Penny and Trudy that Kat would be staying with him until the storm cleared and they were safe and snug inside the cabin.

But instead of resting assured, Jack's pulse skittered in an agitated, erratic rhythm. The cozy, intimate environment seemed to be lowering their walls and inhibitions. And the vulnerability made him feel at once wary and wonderful.

Carrying their hot chocolate back to the couch, he asked, "Would you like to watch a Christmas movie?"

"Sure. That sounds fun."

"Any favorites?"

"Do you have *Holiday Inn*?"

Jack stumbled on the edge of the carpet, barely preventing the steaming hot beverage from winding up in her lap. Gulping a sigh of relief, he carefully set both mugs on the coffee table. "Yeah, I do. My sister and I watch it every year."

"Oh, I don't want to hijack a tradition. We can watch something else."

"No, it's okay. I'd like to watch it with you." The words left his lips before the sentiment had fully evolved in his mind. But the spontaneity didn't make them any less true. And he knew Lucy would understand. Especially since she wouldn't be visiting this year, anyway.

While he set up the DVD player, Kat tucked her feet beneath her, arranging the blanket with enough room to share. Jack hid a smile, pretending he hadn't noticed the gesture.

"You and your sister must be close," Kat said as she reached for her mug.

"We try to stay in touch even though she lives several hours away."

"Is it just the two of you?"

"No, I'm the eldest of six. Four brothers and one sister. She's the baby of the family."

"What was it like growing up with so many siblings?"

"Loud. Chaotic. Messy. But also great."

"Sounds wonderful," she said wistfully. "Are you close with your other siblings as well?"

Jack paused, contemplating how to respond as he turned on the TV. Gray static filled the screen before he switched to the proper channel. "Not anymore. My brothers all work for my father's real estate company. Each one's in charge of a different region. Ever since my father and I had a falling out, the relationship between me and my brothers has faded into nonexistence. It's like, as long as my father and I are at odds, the rest of us are in limbo, avoiding the conflict."

"I'm sorry," she said kindly. "Is there hope for you and your father to patch things up?"

Grabbing the DVD remote, Jack stared at it thoughtfully as he mulled over her question. He didn't want to sound too morose, but he answered honestly, "I don't think so."

Cradling her warm mug in her lap, she gazed at him softly, a sympathetic sadness in her eyes.

He didn't want to be pitied. The situation was what it was, and he'd come to grips with it a long time ago.

Attempting to alleviate the mood, he clicked play on the remote, striding toward the sofa. "Ready for the greatest Christmas movie of all time?"

Kat grinned, then her smile faltered. "You're sure your sister won't mind if you watch it without her?"

"One hundred percent." In fact, Jack suspected she'd be glad he finally had a woman on his couch who wasn't his little sister.

Now that he thought about it, he felt certain Lucy would like Kat almost as much as he did. An image of the three of them watching the movie together flooded his mind, but he quickly dismissed it.

There wasn't any point in daydreaming about Kat meeting his sister.

Their paths would never cross.

Lucy wasn't coming home for Christmas.

And Kat would be leaving soon… whether he liked it or not.

CHAPTER 13

The next morning, Kat woke feeling more refreshed than she had in a long time. Jack's bed, piled high with thick, cozy blankets, had created a snug cocoon, and the plaid pajamas he'd loaned her still carried his scent.

She raised her arm, burying her nose in the soft sleeve. But she could barely make out the lingering notes of cedar and chicory as the aroma of freshly brewed coffee and sizzling bacon flooded the bedroom.

Throwing back the covers, Kat slipped from between the flannel sheets, grateful Jack's wool socks protected her feet from the cold hardwood floor.

As she padded softly down the narrow hallway, a sharp bark startled her. Instantly concerned, she dashed into the living room, her pulse racing. "What's wrong? Is Fitz okay?"

"We've adopted quite the beggar," Jack said with a chuckle.

Her heart sputtered at his use of *we*, but she tried not to read into it.

As though he'd transformed overnight, Fitz sat on his haunches, his furry backside wiggling in excitement as Jack dangled a strip of bacon.

"Let's show Bennet what you learned." Holding out his free hand, Jack commanded, "Shake."

To Kat's surprise, Fitz placed his large paw in Jack's open palm.

"Good boy," Jack praised before tossing the reward.

Fitz caught it midair, gobbling it down with gusto.

Kat smiled as she watched the adorable exchange. "I'm impressed. You just taught him that?"

"He's a quick study."

When he'd finished scarfing down his reward, the pup trotted over to Kat, nudging her leg with his muzzle.

"Good morning to you, too," she laughed, scratching behind his fluffy ears.

"What'd I tell you? He's a beggar." Grabbing a long, ivory object from the counter, he offered it to the dog. "Here, buddy. Try this."

Fitz sniffed it a moment before taking it gently from Jack's hand. Prancing toward his bed by the fire, he stretched out on the blanket and began gnawing on his new treat.

"What was that?" Kat asked, sliding onto a barstool at the generous island. She noticed the kitchen seemed particularly well equipped given the modest size of the cabin.

"It's a deer antler. My sister gave it to me as some sort of decoration last Christmas. She studied interior design and has made it her mission to improve my *bachelor pad*, as she calls it."

Kat glanced around the sparse space, noting the obvious lack of cohesive style. Unless *minimalist lumberjack* counted as a style. "She has her work cut out for her," she teased.

He laughed—deep and rumbling. She found the sound comforting, like the murmur of a warm, inviting fire. And for a fleeting moment, she wondered if Jack could sing. His voice carried a certain richness and clarity common in skilled vocalists —a quality her mother had possessed in spades. But she quickly pushed the thought aside, not wanting unpleasant memories to dampen the mood.

"No argument there," he confessed with a grin. "And she does her best. But I'm not into knickknacks. However, it makes an excellent chew toy for my new houseguest."

With his bushy tail fluttering like a feather duster, Fitz appeared more than happy to take the trinket off Jack's hands.

"Any luck finding his owner?"

"I made a few calls this morning." Jack poured steaming, aromatic coffee into two mugs, and asked, "How do you take it?"

"Black is perfect, thanks."

He slid the mug toward her. "It seems no one in town owns a dog that matches Fitz's description."

"So, you're keeping him?" She couldn't help the hopeful tremor in her voice.

Jack gazed at the ball of white fluff with affection. "What can I say? He grows on you."

"He sure does. And he seems to have recovered overnight."

"I guess all he needed was a good meal and a warm place to sleep. Speaking of which, how did you sleep?"

"Like a baby. You?"

"Never better."

She hid a smile behind the rim of her mug, knowing that couldn't be true. He'd opted to sleep on the couch by Fitz rather than the guest house, so he could keep an eye on the pup throughout the night. And he'd insisted she take his room since it was the most comfortable.

As Jack resumed fixing breakfast, Kat took a sip of coffee, recognizing the hints of cinnamon and caramel as it warmed her throat. "This is Cassie's Christmas Morning blend, isn't it?"

"It is, but if you tell anyone I drink froufrou flavored coffee, I'll deny it with my last breath."

"My lips are sealed," she laughed, noticing the way he poured the pancake batter with a practiced hand. "Why don't you serve breakfast at the diner? You obviously know what you're doing."

He didn't respond right away, creating perfect circles of batter on the round cast-iron skillet. "I usually tell people it's because we're busy enough as it is."

"That isn't true?"

"It's true, but it isn't the main reason."

Kat sipped her coffee, savoring each scintillating flavor note, waiting for him to continue.

"I cooked my first meal completely on my own when I was ten years old. My parents had both started jobs early in the morning, which left me in charge of breakfast."

"What did you make?"

"Flapjacks and bacon. On this very skillet, actually." A wistful expression stole over him as he studied the tiny bubbles perforating the thick batter. "I loved making breakfast for my family. And flapjacks in particular are still sentimental. They remind me of when life was simple and full of joy, before my parents' obsession with wealth and status ruined everything." His features clouded a moment, and Kat wondered how deep his wounds with his family ran.

But his countenance quickly brightened as he seemed to shake the unpleasant memories loose with a smile. "Now I only like to make them for special people in my life. Doing it for work would lose some of the magic, as sappy as that sounds. Of course, now that I talked them up so much, I better not burn them, huh?" He chuckled, flipping one over with an expert flick of his wrist.

Kat sat in breathless silence, not knowing what to say.

Had Jack just referred to her as someone special?

*a*s Jack slid the heaping mound of food in front of Kat, his heart pounded inside his chest. What if she didn't like it? What if he'd accidentally added too much salt or nutmeg? He should have made a test batch first.

"Are you going to join me? Or stand there and stare at me while I eat?" she asked with a teasing lilt.

Flustered, Jack cleared his throat. After grabbing a fork from the silverware drawer, he hopped on the barstool next to her, facing the kitchen window.

The world beyond the frosted glass sparkled in the sunlight, making every snow-covered surface appear as though it had been encrusted with a million melee diamonds.

Out of the corner of his eye, he watched Kat drizzle maple syrup over her stack of flapjacks while he nibbled on a strip of crisp bacon, barely tasting the smoky, applewood flavor.

As she brought the first bite to her lips, his breath lodged in his throat.

She chewed—agonizingly slow—until she finally swallowed. To his relief, a smile danced on her lips as she said, "It's a shame you don't serve breakfast. I'd eat at the diner every morning if this were on the menu."

A goofy grin stretched across his face, but he didn't care. "Every morning, huh? If that's what it takes to keep you in town, I might consider it."

A pretty blush dusted her cheeks, giving him the courage to continue. "I was thinking… since this is your first snow day, you have some catching up to do."

"What do you mean?"

"You've never gone sledding, made a snow angel, or had a snowball fight."

"That's true…." She raised one eyebrow as though curious to see where he was going with his observation.

"Instead of rushing back into town, I thought we'd check a few things off the list. What do you say? Are you game?"

She hesitated a moment, dragging her fork through a puddle of syrup. "Okay," she said at last, with a twinge of reservation.

"Great!" he cheered with enough enthusiasm for the both of them.

"But I have to warn you," she added, her green eyes glinting playfully. "You'll probably lose the snowball fight."

"Is that so?"

"After several years of Krav Maga, I have a tactical advantage. Frankly, you don't stand a chance."

"Is that a challenge?"

"May the best woman win." She smirked as she raised her mug in a salute.

"Challenge accepted." As he clinked his cup against hers, he realized he meant far more than winning a snowball fight.

CHAPTER 14

*K*at couldn't believe she'd spent the morning at Jack's rather than racing to Penny's with the answer to the riddle. To think, she could be holding the brooch in her hands right now.

Perhaps she'd even be on her way back to Starcross Cove.

Instead, she found herself hiding behind a stout tree trunk clutching a perfectly packed snowball in her gloved hand. And she didn't regret her decision for a second.

Peeking around the scratchy bark, she squinted through the thicket of redwood trees behind Jack's cabin hoping to glimpse his bright blue jacket. Although his large, muscular frame and choice in snow gear was anything but subtle, she couldn't spot him anywhere.

While she stood watch, she absentmindedly smoothed the puffy down filling of the trendy Moncler ski jacket that belonged to Jack's sister, Lucy. Kat didn't think she'd ever worn anything so expensive in all her life. The coat itself probably cost more than her entire wardrobe back home. Not to mention the luxury of leaving behind snow gear for one visit a year.

Kat briefly wondered what Lucy was like. From Jack's

description, she seemed his opposite in every way. And yet, he clearly adored her. Curiously, whenever he spoke of his little sister, a hint of melancholy hid behind his affectionate expression and Kat longed to know what it meant.

A cheerful bark interrupted her musings as Fitz bounded through the snow toward her. The pup had enjoyed the morning almost as much as she had, racing behind their sleds and rollicking in the soft white powder as they made snow angels, occasionally licking Jack's face.

"What is it, boy?" She bent down to pet the thick, bushy fur around his neck.

Whack!

A snowball splattered against the tree trunk inches from her head, scattering icy flecks down the collar of her jacket. She whirled around to face her attacker, laughter in her eyes. "Ha! You missed!"

"Only because Fitz warned you, the traitor."

Fitz wagged his tail in response.

"Good boy," she cooed, patting the top of his head.

"We'll discuss this later," Jack told the dog with mock sternness.

"You're out of ammunition. What are you going to do now?" she asked, her hand poised, ready to fire.

An impish smile curled his lips and his eyes narrowed like a scope zeroing in on its target. "It's time for guerrilla warfare."

Kat shrieked gleefully as he ran toward her with a look that said he had every intention of tackling her into a snowdrift. She sprinted for the open field, laughter trailing behind her.

Fitz joined in the fun by nipping at Jack's heels, his excited bark echoing through the trees.

Still several yards from the cabin, Kat quickly planned her attack as Jack's long strides spanned the distance between them. In a matter of seconds, he'd reach her.

Gently tossing the snowball nearby, Kat waited for Jack to

close the gap, and in a deft, fluid movement that befit her years of training, she flipped him onto his back in a dense mound of snow.

He stared up at her, wide-eyed and winded.

Plucking the snowball from its resting place, she knelt over him, armed and ready. "Do you surrender?"

His gaze fell to her mouth, stealing the smirk from her lips.

Something about the way he looked at her—both soft and intense—left her momentarily breathless. Was he about to kiss her?

Before she knew what was happening, he'd rolled over, pinning her on her back.

"Do *you?*" he asked, his face mere centimeters from her own.

Overcome with the sudden urge to press her lips against his, Kat did the only thing she could—she kneed him in the side and wriggled to safety.

"Oof!" Jack clutched his stomach as he toppled over.

Scrambling to her feet, Kat blurted, "I'm so sorry!" as her pulse pounded in her ears.

"Don't tell me," he moaned. "Your instincts kicked in?"

She offered a sheepish smile as she helped him to his feet. "After a decade of training, it's a hard habit to break." She decided not to mention the part about her unsettling attraction. Or her desperate need to escape before she did something impulsive and possibly regrettable.

"I might need some hot chocolate to soothe the pain."

"I think I can manage that."

What she *couldn't* manage were her growing feelings for Jack.

Or how deeply her heart would break when it came time to say goodbye.

*a*s Jack watched Kat prepare the hot chocolate with such delicate, graceful movements, he marveled at how only moments ago she'd dropped him in a snowdrift like a sack of potatoes.

If he were honest, he found it impressive and incredibly attractive.

"You're quite the expert at—what did you call it?"

"Krav Maga?"

"Yeah, that's it. Have you thought about going into law enforcement or something? With skills like that, you'd be a real asset. I'd trust you to have my back, that's for sure."

"Thanks."

Jack caught her pleased smile before she reached into the cupboard for two mugs. Although she'd been inside his cabin for less than forty-eight hours, she already seemed to know where he kept everything. And she moved about the space as effortlessly as if she were in her own home—a realization that secretly thrilled him.

"But I'd never leave Hope Hideaway," she added, instantly deflating his elation. "Fern needs me."

He slouched on the barstool, his heart sinking. How could he argue with that? He admired her loyalty. And yet, he couldn't help grasping for straws. "In another life, where would you live? What would you want to do?"

She hesitated as though his line of questioning made her uncomfortable. "In another life?" she repeated slowly.

"Purely hypothetical."

"Well..." With a contemplative expression, she poured the rich, silky liquid into two stoneware mugs. "I always thought it would be fun to own an inn."

"Like the Morning Glory Inn?"

"Yes, only with more rooms and enough space to hold work-shops and art classes and even have its own restaurant."

As she spoke, her entire face illuminated from within, and her passion was almost palpable.

"Any idea where you'd want the inn to be located?" he asked, praying she'd say Poppy Creek. Although, he knew his wish was ridiculous.

"Not really. The fantasy never evolved to logistics."

"When did you first have the idea?"

She settled on the barstool beside him, but faced the living room where Fitz lounged on the couch, chewing his antler. Just like Kat, the pup had made himself at home. And for a brief moment, Jack basked in the glow of what it felt like to have a family again.

"Honestly," Kat continued, "the thought first came to me during a conversation with my friend Maxine. She'd been staying at Hope Hideaway for a few months, trying to get back on her feet after rehab. She told me the shelter was the closest thing she'd had to a vacation in her entire life."

"Really?" Jack responded in surprise. "Not even a weekend trip somewhere?"

"She didn't have the most glamorous life."

He nodded in understanding, appreciating that she couldn't go into the details.

She took a long sip before confessing, "It made me realize how many people don't have the opportunity to stay somewhere nice—to sleep in a luxurious bed, eat delicious food, and spend a few days away from it all."

His heart melted at the compassion coating her every word.

"I know it wouldn't change the world or anything, but I'd like to own a place where the best room is reserved for people like Maxine. Which, I realize, might sound frivolous when there are bigger problems to solve."

"It's not frivolous," he said in earnest.

A look passed between them that stopped his heart from beating, but she abruptly shrugged and averted her gaze. "It's just a silly dream, though. It'll never happen."

"Why not?" He leaned forward, suddenly desperate to make her dream come true.

"For starters, I'd never have the means for something like that. And secondly, as I mentioned earlier, I couldn't leave Fern."

As Jack let the reality of her words sink in, an idea began to take shape.

While he couldn't solve the second problem, he might have a solution to the first one.

CHAPTER 15

"Come in, come in." Penny held the door open for Kat to slip past her. "I snuffed out the fire as soon as you called, but the bricks inside the hearth are still a little too hot." She wrapped her beaded shawl tighter around her shoulders. "Can I make you some tea? It's starting to get chilly in here."

"Tea would be great, thanks."

Kat sat cross-legged on the floor near Chip, missing Fitz's company already. She smiled as the tortoise waddled toward her, extending his wrinkled neck so she could nuzzle his head with the tip of her finger.

"I may have to go downstairs if we hear the bell above the entrance, but it's been a slow day thanks to the storm." Penny filled an antique copper kettle with water from the sink and set it on the stove. "I'm so glad you were able to solve the riddle. I was beginning to wonder if we'd ever figure it out."

"Actually, Jack deserves the credit. It only took him a few seconds to solve, too."

"Really?" Penny elongated each syllable, showcasing her curiosity. "What was it like? Getting trapped together in the snowstorm, I mean."

Kat blushed as her sister filled an infuser with fragrant tea leaves, watching her closely. "It was… uneventful."

Penny pinched her eyebrows together as if she didn't quite believe her, but she didn't press further, busying herself with arranging gingersnaps on a dainty china plate. "I guess it must've taken a while for the roads to clear this morning."

Kat's blush deepened as though she were a toddler caught stealing Santa's milk and cookies. She really needed to switch topics, but nothing else came to mind. She couldn't steer her thoughts away from Jack no matter how hard she tried.

Hoping for a distraction, she turned her attention back to Chip, but he'd shuffled toward his enclosure, apparently uninterested in their girl talk.

"You know, Jack hasn't had a girlfriend since high school," Penny informed her out of the blue.

"Oh?" She tried—unsuccessfully—to keep the interest out of her voice.

Penny's lips twitched and she opened her mouth to say more, but the kettle screeched, cutting her off, much to Kat's dismay. She waited impatiently as Penny filled the teapot with boiling water. Could she pour any slower?

"Her name was Ashley Tanner," Penny said at last, carrying the plate of cookies to the coffee table. "We were all waiting for Jack to propose, but one day she simply packed her bags and left town, almost like she'd vanished into thin air. It was strange."

"Were you two friends?" Kat asked, wanting to know all she could about the woman Jack almost married.

"Not friends, per se." She sank onto the chaise lounge, the fringe of her shawl draped elegantly across the teal velvet upholstery. "She was always nice to me, but she was a few years older than I was and, honestly, fairly intimidating."

Kat's stomach twisted. Of course she was. What else did she expect?

As if noticing her crestfallen expression, Penny quickly added, "But she wasn't right for Jack."

"Why do you say that?"

"It's hard to explain. It was an intangible quality. I always got the sense that Poppy Creek wasn't enough for her. Which made me wonder if *Jack* would be enough for her."

Kat straightened, suddenly indignant at the notion that Jack was somehow lacking in anything. She started to protest, but caught her sister's somber countenance. "What's wrong?"

"It's just…" Penny hesitated before adding softly, "It made me think of Helena and how love wasn't enough for her, either."

Her chest tightening, Kat looked away, focusing on the landscape painting above the mantel—the emerald green hills seemed to disappear into the indigo horizon with one effortless brushstroke.

As if sensing her discomfort, Penny mustered up a smile. "The tea should be ready." Rising from the chaise lounge, she strode the few feet into the kitchen.

Desperate to change the subject, Kat said, "You have lovely artwork."

"Thank you. Dad collected most of it. In fact"—her face brightened—"there's one I want to show you." She motioned for Kat to join her in the kitchen. "This one is my favorite."

Although the photograph had clearly been taken decades earlier, Kat instantly recognized the stately home perched on a bluff overlooking the ocean. "That's Hope Hideaway." Her gaze traveled the well-known path to the beach, resting on two small girls building a sandcastle. The youngest couldn't have been more than two years old. Her breath stalled. "Is that—"

"It's the two of us. My dad took it the day he brought me to Starcross Cove, hoping to win Helena back. After all those years, he'd never stopped loving her." Penny's voice trembled, and Kat struggled to keep her own emotions under control.

"I don't remember," she whispered, grazing the edge of the wooden frame with her fingertip.

"We were too young. But now we can make new memories together." Penny turned to face her, her eyes shimmering.

Kat's throat burned and she found it difficult to swallow. This woman had been nothing but kind, and yet Kat couldn't even tell her the truth about their mother's death. Not without facing feelings she'd long suppressed.

"Gosh, listen to me." Penny sniffled. "I'm standing here blubbering when we have a brooch to find." Smiling through her unshed tears, she led the way to the fireplace, cautiously testing the temperature of the bricks.

Kat followed, uncertain if she should regret or rejoice that the moment had passed.

"I think they're cool enough," Penny announced, running a finger along the crumbling grout. "If this is anything like the movies, there's a loose brick here somewhere."

Joining her sister, Kat felt along the grooves, her heart beating faster as they searched.

"I found it!" Penny cried after several minutes of combing every inch of the firebox.

Kat held her breath as Penny carefully slid the brick from its slot, the sound of scraping clay filling the suspenseful silence.

She expected to see a small pouch or trinket box inside, but instead, another square of paper stared back at them, sullied and singed around the edges.

"Oh, Kat. I'm so sorry," Penny murmured as she removed the next clue. "I really thought we'd find the brooch this time."

Kat pressed her lips into a thin line, words failing her. Instead of disappointment, her heart had filled with relief. But she couldn't pinpoint the reason. Or rather, she couldn't admit it— even to herself.

Penny shook flecks of ash from the note before carefully

unfolding the corners. "I can't believe it survived in there for so long."

"Considering your dad planned all of this for your Christmas break, I imagine he only meant for it to be hidden for a few days. What does it say?"

"'A tale as old as time, a love beyond refrain, a story penned in rhyme, a rose by any name.'" Beaming, Penny cried in excitement, "I know this one!"

"You do?" Kat asked, surprised she'd solved it so quickly.

"It's *Romeo and Juliet!*" Dashing across the room, Penny dropped to her knees in front of a short bookcase stuffed with leather-bound classics. She thumbed across the embossed spines until she landed on a burgundy binding with navy lettering.

"Where would he hide a brooch inside a book?" Kat asked, kneeling beside her.

"A false backing, maybe? A hollow spine?" Penny ran her hand along every inch of the worn surface, finally shaking the book like a piggy bank.

Nothing happened.

Penny frowned. "I don't understand. The riddle has to be about *Romeo and Juliet*. Everything fits."

"It was a good guess." Kat offered a sympathetic smile. "With a bit more time, I'm sure we'll figure it out."

"You're right," Penny sighed. "And I confess, I'm happy you'll be staying a little while longer. Tonight's Pajama Christmas."

"What's Pajama Christmas?"

"It's our tree-lighting ceremony. Every December 6, we—" The faint twinkling of a bell interrupted her answer.

"Hang on." Penny sprang to her feet. "I'll be right back."

In her sister's absence, Kat meandered to the coffee table where they'd left their tea and took a sip. Though lukewarm, she savored the subtle notes of vanilla and cloves while she wandered back to the photograph in the kitchen. She still couldn't comprehend all the ethereal threads connecting their pasts.

Lost in her thoughts, Kat nearly spilled the tea down the front of her sweater when Penny returned moments later, taking her by surprise.

"Sorry, I didn't mean to startle you." Penny cradled a large package in her arms.

"What's that?" Kat asked.

"I don't know." With a curious expression, Penny handed her the box. "It's for you."

*S*urreptitiously, Jack closed his office door so no one in the kitchen would overhear his phone call. Stealing to his desk, he flipped through his old-fashioned Rolodex for the number of his financial advisor.

Paul Volt picked up after the first ring. "Jack! What can I do for my favorite client?"

Grinning, Jack kicked back in his chair. He knew for a fact he was one of Paul's only clients. But considering the amount of money Jack paid him to handle his finances, he didn't need many. Of course, Jack would've gladly paid him ten times his monthly retainer fee to avoid dealing with gobs of money he didn't need, courtesy of a successful business and a simple lifestyle. Out of sight, out of mind was how he preferred it.

"Hey, Paul. Do you remember the property my dad gave me several years ago?"

"The old mansion on Windsor?"

"Yep, that's the one."

"Sure. What about it?"

"I want you to look into the zoning for me. Specifically, what it would take to turn it into an inn."

"You want to run an inn?" Paul didn't bother hiding his aston-ishment.

"Something like that," Jack said cryptically. "How long until you can have some information for me?"

"I'll get started this afternoon." Still sounding incredulous, Paul bid him goodbye before ending the call.

Leaning forward, Jack placed the cordless phone on the receiver, shaking his head in amusement. He didn't blame Paul for being confused. Ever since his father had gifted him the property, Jack had let it sit stagnant. The bold-faced bribe had been like salt in a still-gaping wound.

Revisiting the painful memories wouldn't be easy.

But for Kat? It would be worth it.

CHAPTER 16

*a*s Kat stepped onto Main Street, her breath hitched at the beautiful sight before her. The entire town square dazzled beneath a canopy of twinkling lights. Every speck of snow had been cleared from the streets and the center lawn, but it still capped the rooftops and tree branches, adding to the magical, glittery effect.

Townspeople clad in wintry and festive-themed pajamas gathered around blazing firepits or huddled beneath the amber glow of heat lamps.

Kat pulled her vintage chenille robe tighter around her, although she didn't cinch the waist, allowing just enough of the elegant 1950s nightgown to peek through. She'd had her reservations when Penny explained the quirky tradition, but she'd underestimated its charm. Now that she saw the event up close, she was absolutely smitten with it.

Kat scanned the bright, jovial faces in the crowd, searching for one in particular. Since he stood several inches taller than everyone else, he wasn't hard to spot. Her stomach fluttered when she noticed Jack's gaze followed the same sweeping pattern as her own. Could he be looking for her?

THE MEANING IN MISTLETOE

Their eyes locked, and a heart-stopping smile illuminated his features, warming Kat all the way down to her toes. Something was definitely happening between them, and she couldn't deny wanting to discover whatever *it* was. In all her life, she'd never experienced so much joy and exhilaration wrapped in equal amounts of anxious trepidation.

Gathering her nerves, she inhaled deeply, catching a whiff of her new perfume. She still couldn't believe Fern had mailed her the package filled with clothing, makeup, a few personal items, and the early Christmas present.

Fern's note had simply stated that she'd spotted the perfume bottle in a shop window and couldn't resist. Of course, Kat shouldn't have been surprised Fern knew exactly where to send it. The woman had an uncanny knack for knowing the unknowable. In truth, she'd probably written the return address down the minute she received Penny's letter. And all that talk of moldy cheese and *A Christmas Carol* had been a not-so-subtle push for Kat to finally visit her sister.

As for the perfume... Well, Kat couldn't wait to wear it for Jack. It wasn't fruity or floral, she had a feeling he wouldn't appreciate those scents. Instead, it smelled warm and sultry with hints of spicy cardamom and saffron wrapped in woodsy amber.

With an unwavering gaze, Jack strode straight toward her, and Kat stifled a laugh as he emerged through the crowd. The man confidently wore a red onesie paired with a fur-lined trapper hat and shiny black boots.

"Did you steal Santa's pajamas?" she teased, trying not to gawk at the way his substantial biceps strained the ribbed cotton fabric.

"They're on loan." He grinned, but his features immediately softened as he drank her in. "Wow. You look—"

"Ridiculous?" She self-consciously tugged the delicate lace of the Peter Pan collar.

"You look great." Based on his expression, she suspected his words were an understatement, and her cheeks flushed.

"You made it!" Interrupting their intimate exchange, Penny joined them, beaming at Kat. "Your outfit looks amazing!"

"It should. You picked it out," Kat said with a laugh. Her sister looked adorable in a quilted robe and flannel nightgown, her long auburn hair bundled in a scrunchie on top of her head.

"True." Penny grinned. "And Jack, the only person who can top your getup is Colt. He insisted on wearing the pink bunny pajamas from *A Christmas Story*."

"He would," Jack snorted in amusement.

Penny's eyes lit up when she spotted someone across the square. "Oh, look! Frank and Beverly are here. I've been dying to introduce you. You two get in line for hot chocolate, and I'll bring them over."

As her sister skipped across the lawn, Kat couldn't help noticing how the entire town buzzed with merriment.

"This is quite the tradition," she said as they walked toward the quaint hot chocolate stand nestled between two booths, one serving roasted chestnuts and the other a variety of candied caramel corn.

"It's my favorite holiday event. When Mayor Burns lights the tree, we all sing Christmas carols. You're going to love it."

"Oh, I don't sing."

"You don't sing?" As he cocked his head, the ear flaps of his hat flopped to one side. "I'm sure you don't sound *that* bad."

"I didn't say I *can't* sing. I said I don't sing."

"Why not?"

Kat hesitated. She'd never told anyone, not even Fern, but for some reason, she wanted to share with Jack—an impulse she had given up questioning.

"Well—" she began, pausing when a flicker of shock darted across his face.

Following his gaze, she saw a stunning raven-haired woman

sashayed toward them. The exotic beauty would have stood out in any situation, but in her sleek, black leather pants, high-heeled boots and trendy, camel-colored car coat, she was impossible to miss.

"Ashley?"

Even though the woman's name escaped Jack's lips in a strangled whisper, they bulldozed Kat like a runaway sleigh.

❄

"*J*ack Gardener, aren't you a sight for sore eyes?"

A chill ran down Jack's spine as Ashley looked him over with a provocative glint in her dark obsidian eyes. They looked the same, yet different—every bit as mesmerizing but more worldly and less warm.

"Ashley." He nearly choked on her name and hastily cleared his throat. "What are you doing here?"

"Jack." She sighed like a patient schoolteacher. "Aren't you going to introduce me to your friend?"

His glaze flew to Kat. Her features had gone pale. "Ashley, this is Kat. Kat, this is Ashley."

"Nice to meet you." Ashley extended her hand, and Kat shook it, dazed and speechless. "You don't mind if I borrow him for a moment, do you?"

Kat shook her head, still not speaking.

"Actually, we're in the middle of a conversation," Jack told her, not wanting to leave Kat's side for even a second. Especially not with her.

"Surely you can spare two minutes for an old friend."

He didn't like the way she said *friend* with so much emphasis. "Maybe later."

"Don't be silly. Kat doesn't mind." She coiled her fingers around his arm. "I promise to bring him back in one piece."

What was that supposed to mean? Jack stiffened as she

hooked her hand in the crook of his elbow and steered him away from Kat. "I see you're just as stubborn as ever." Her voice carried the same playful lilt that he remembered, but it didn't melt his heart the way it used to.

"What are you doing here?" he repeated, shrugging his arm from her grasp.

"Can't a girl come home for Christmas?"

"This isn't your home. You made that clear when you left. And you can't be visiting your parents since they retired in Florida. So, what really brings you back to Poppy Creek?"

"The truth?"

He folded his arms in front of his chest.

"I heard you were inquiring into the Windsor property."

Jack straightened, his hands falling to his sides. "How'd you hear about that?"

"I know everything there is to know about that house. Your dad made it part of my job to stay informed."

Seething, Jack tried to keep his anger in check, pressing his fingertips into his palm. Of course his father would have his ex-girlfriend keep tabs on him. It wasn't enough that he'd lured her away after Jack turned down his job offer, knowing full well he'd already bought her a ring. The entire scenario still made him sick to his stomach.

"So, you flew all the way out here from New York to... what? See if the rumors were true?" If his father thought that Jack finally doing something with the property meant he'd forgiven him—or worse, wanted anything to do with the company—he was in for a surprise.

"Jack, I'm living in LA now. I thought Lucy told you."

"Lucy? Why would she know anything about it?"

She stared at him with a puzzled expression. "Because we're working together. We have been for several months. Honestly, Jack, I thought you knew."

Every light, color, and sound blurred together as her words trampled over him.

And in that moment, Jack wasn't sure if he knew anything anymore.

CHAPTER 17

*S*unlight tiptoed through the gap in the curtains, tempting Kat to greet the new day. With a groan, she yanked the covers over her head, refusing to stir from the comfort of the silky soft sheets.

Today, she'd committed to meet up with Jack to finish the display. But how could she face him after how she'd behaved last night? He'd tried to reconnect after his conversation with Ashley, but Kat had avoided him, an immature reaction at best.

Seeing Jack with his ex had forced her to confront the depth of her feelings for him. Not to mention the foolishness of falling for someone who lived hundreds of miles away. What was she thinking?

Clearly, she wasn't. And that was the problem.

The tantalizing aroma of Belgian waffles wafted into the bedroom, reminding Kat that she'd promised Trudy she'd join them for breakfast.

After shoving the covers aside, she hastily dressed and trudged down the staircase, attempting to rouse a dollop of enthusiasm.

"Good morning, dearie!" Trudy set a glass jar of homemade

strawberry preserves on the artfully arranged dining table brimming with enough food to feed Santa's entire workshop. "We're thrilled you could join us."

As Kat eased herself onto one of the floral-upholstered dining chairs, she noticed the smiling couple sitting across from her.

"Kat, I'd like you to meet Elle and Graham Dalton." Trudy's delight was evident in the soft creases around her eyes. "They first stayed with us last spring, and I told them they simply had to come back at Christmastime." A timer trilled, and she clapped her hands. "The muffins are ready!"

As Trudy dashed into the kitchen, the pretty young woman smiled warmly at Kat. "Trudy made Christmas in Poppy Creek sound so idyllic, we couldn't think of a better place to spend our honeymoon. Plus, we're also here for a friend's wedding."

Great. Newlyweds. Just what she needed when her heart felt like it had been trampled by a herd of reindeer. "Congratulations."

"Thank you. Coffee?" Elle passed her a ceramic carafe.

"Yes, please." Kat filled her mug to the brim, ignoring the way the couple subtly leaned toward each other as though their chairs weren't close enough already. Or the way Graham kept casting adoring glances in his wife's direction as if the way she buttered her toast deserved a standing ovation.

She stared down at her own plate of perfectly plump and golden waffles. Who would've thought such a mouthwatering meal could leave her feeling so melancholy?

"So, Kat," Elle began, apparently intent on small talk. "Trudy says you're in town visiting your sister."

"Yes, I am." For some reason, the ability to make lively conversation had escaped her.

"How long are you staying?" Graham asked, scooping a heaping spoonful of strawberry preserves onto his generous stack of syrup-soaked waffles.

"That's... undecided."

The newlyweds exchanged a confused glance as Kat sipped her coffee.

"She's on a treasure hunt," Trudy announced with a grand, mysterious air as she placed a basket of warm poppyseed muffins in the center of the table.

Kat sputtered, wiping the dribbles of coffee off her chin with the back of her hand. "How did you know that?"

"It's a small town, dear," Trudy said as though it explained everything.

"A treasure hunt? How fun." Elle sounded intrigued.

"With a map?" Graham asked.

Kat shook her head. "Riddles, actually."

"I love riddles." An older man with thinning silvery hair and tanned sun-wrinkled skin burst from the kitchen carrying a tray of sizzling sausage and bacon. Although they hadn't officially met, Kat recognized him as Trudy's husband, George. "Can you share one of the clues with us?" He sat at the head of the table, while Trudy took the chair to his right.

"Sure." Kat wouldn't turn down extra help. And luckily, this one had been easier to memorize. "The most recent one is 'A tale as old as time, a love beyond refrain, a story penned in rhyme, a rose by any name.'"

"*Romeo and Juliet?*" Graham guessed almost immediately. "It's a classic love story, an eternal romance in which Shakespeare utilizes rhyming couplets. And in the second act, Juliet says, 'What's in a name? That which we call a rose, by any other name would smell as sweet.'"

"Graham always aced our high school English exams." Elle gifted her husband with a proud, doting smile.

"That's what my sister, Penny, guessed as well. But when we checked her copy of *Romeo and Juliet*, we couldn't find anything."

Everyone's brow furrowed in thought, their breakfast forgotten.

"What about an adaptation?" Graham asked.

"Yes!" Elle snapped her fingers. "Like *West Side Story*." She grinned sheepishly as she added, "I watched the movie in high school instead of reading the play."

"That's an interesting idea," Kat said slowly. "I did notice a shelf of old DVDs. It's worth a look."

"Will you let us know if you find it?" Elle asked.

"Absolutely," Kat told her as they all resumed eating.

She caught the newlyweds exchange another loving glance and her stomach twisted.

Until meeting Jack, she'd resigned herself to remaining single forever, like Fern.

But now, she wasn't sure what she wanted anymore.

"*C*ome on, Luce. Pick up," Jack muttered before the call went to voice mail. He'd been trying to reach her all morning, but she was either avoiding him or busy. He hoped it was the latter.

"Knock, knock." Vick ducked his head into the office. "Someone's here to see you."

"Thanks. I'll be right there." Jack stood, his heart pounding. He hadn't seen Kat since last night when she'd remained glued to Penny's side. Come to think of it, she'd acted strange ever since Ashley showed up. Hopefully, she hadn't read too much into it. And if so, he'd gladly set the record straight while they worked on the display this afternoon.

Passing through the busy kitchen, Jack stepped into the main dining area, already wearing a grin in anticipation of seeing Kat again.

"My, aren't you in a good mood today."

His blood chilled at the sight of his ex. "You're still in town?"

She ignored his comment. "Rumor has it you want to turn the Windsor house into an inn. Is that true?"

"Maybe." He folded his arms in front of his chest, on the defensive. "Why do you care?"

"I can help you."

"Isn't it a little presumptuous to assume I'd even want your help? We haven't spoken in years."

"You act like that's my fault."

"I'm not the one who left." His jaw clenched, and he hated that she had this effect on him. He suspected his feelings for Ashley had gotten tangled up in his anger toward his father. Either way, he didn't want to be having this conversation in the middle of his crowded diner.

"But you're the one who didn't come after me." She pinned him with her dark, piercing eyes as though she planned to gaze right into his soul.

But he wouldn't give her that luxury, not anymore. "You knew I'd never follow you to New York."

"But I'm in Los Angeles now." She walked toward him, the click-clack of her heels matching the throbbing of his temples. "A lot has changed, Jack. You want to open an inn, which is a far cry from when all you wanted was a sleepy diner. It's so ambitious. It's so—"

"Unlike me?" Jack finished for her.

"I didn't say that."

"But you *thought* it, didn't you? You were always disappointed I didn't have loftier goals. I just never knew about it. Until it was too late."

"Jack," she released an exasperated sigh, "does any of this matter anymore? I mean, look at you now." She waved a hand to encompass the bustling restaurant. "It's not even the lunch rush yet and every booth is filled. You've obviously done quite well for yourself. I'll be sure to pass that along to your father," she added pointedly.

"Don't bother," he growled.

"Why not? Don't you want him to know how successful you've become after turning down his job offer?"

"You mean, the job offer *you* took?" He regretted the bitter edge to his words. Especially when he noticed her almost imperceptible wince.

"I just thought you'd want him to know how well you've done." She raised her chin as though reclaiming her aura of impenetrable confidence.

"That's the difference between you and me," he said softly. "I don't care what other people think."

Even as he said the words, he knew they weren't entirely true. He cared what Kat thought. Especially now as she breezed through the front door and spotted him speaking with Ashley in hushed tones. Her eyes widened ever so slightly before she spun around, exiting the way she came.

"I have to go," he said abruptly, brushing past her.

Hurrying outside, he trotted down the sidewalk and tapped Kat's shoulder before throwing up his hands. "Don't attack. I'm unarmed."

This elicited a small smile as she turned to face him. "Sorry, I didn't mean to interrupt your conversation."

"You didn't. In fact, I've been counting down the seconds until you showed up."

She flushed. "Does that mean you're ready to work on the display?"

"Yep. I'm embracing my inner Martha Stewart. Let's go grab the arbor and get started." As they walked around back to the storage shed, Jack stole a sideways glance as he said casually, "We kept missing each other in the crowd last night."

"Yes, I suppose we did," she said without meeting his gaze.

"I thought we'd make up for it tonight."

"What'd you have in mind?" She peered up at him through thick lashes.

"It's a surprise."

"A surprise?"

"Yeah, you do like surprises, don't you?"

"I guess it depends on what it is." She smirked.

"Fair enough," he said with a chuckle. "Normally, the gentlemanly thing would be to pick you up. But what if we meet at my place instead? There's someone there who'd really like to see you."

Her face brightened. "I'd love that. I've missed him."

Jack was tempted to ask if she'd missed him, too, but didn't want to come on too strong.

A faint buzzing sound emanated from somewhere inside her coat pocket. Her expression clouded as soon as she read the text message.

"Everything okay?" he asked.

"Everything's great." She stuffed her phone back inside her pocket and flashed him a heart-stopping smile.

How could one simple gesture make him forget everything? The tension with Ashley. His long-standing family feud. Nothing else seemed to matter in Kat's presence.

And it was the kind of feeling he could get used to.

CHAPTER 18

*A*s Kat stood on Jack's front porch, she marveled that she'd once again chosen spending time with Jack over finding the brooch. It didn't make sense. She *wanted* to find it. And she couldn't wait to tell Fern she'd saved the shelter and finally head home for Christmas.

And yet...

When Penny texted earlier, revealing that she'd found another clue inside the *West Side Story* DVD case—just like Graham and Elle had suggested—Kat should have rushed straight over. Instead, she'd replied with a vague message about things with Jack taking longer than expected and she'd pop by first thing in the morning.

Of course, she hadn't been able to fool her perceptive sister, who'd immediately responded with a winking emoji and an instruction to *have fun*.

Filling her lungs with the frosty night air, Kat knocked in swift succession, matching the brisk beating of her heart.

Jack flung open the front door wearing a grin that made her stomach flip-flop.

Before either of them had a chance to speak, Fitz bounded across the cabin, nearly toppling her over in his excitement.

"It's nice to see you, too," she said with a laugh, kneeling down to bury her face in his thick fur. When she pulled away, she got a face full of doggy kisses.

"Easy, bud," Jack told him with a chuckle. "Have a little dignity."

"Don't you listen to him," Kat purred, scratching behind his ears. "I'm glad you wear your heart on your sleeve."

As she stood, she noticed the cabin smelled like rosemary and garlic. Glancing toward the kitchen, she sucked in a breath.

A plaid tablecloth covered the usually plain dining table. And he'd spruced up a simple place setting for two with fragrant pine branches and holly arranged in a makeshift vase. Beside it, a tea light twinkled inside a clear mason jar.

Astonished, Kat met his gaze.

His eyes held a hesitant glint as he ran his fingers through his hair in a nervous gesture. "I hope you haven't had dinner yet. I thought we'd have a quick bite to eat and hang out with Fitz for a little while before we head out for the evening's main event."

Heat crept up her neck as the reality of the situation unfolded.

Although his original invitation for the evening had sounded more like a casual outing between friends, this most certainly felt like a date.

An intimate date.

The kind of date that might end in a kiss.

✻

*J*ack knew he'd taken a risk not telling Kat about dinner beforehand. Not everyone liked surprises. But based on the pink glow brightening her full cheeks, he'd made the right call.

He only hoped she'd like the next surprise as much as this one.

Last night at Pajama Christmas, she'd confessed she didn't sing. But Jack couldn't imagine a life without it. The pastime had permeated his childhood, providing some of his most cherished memories. More than anything, he wanted a chance to share the experience with Kat. And he felt strongly that she'd enjoy tonight's activity, even as an observer. Although, he prayed for far more than that.

"Whatever you made for dinner smells amazing." She slipped out of her coat, revealing the softest looking emerald-hued sweater he'd ever seen. The richness of the color magnified the intensity of her green eyes in a way that momentarily stole his breath.

"What are we having?" she asked, looping her jacket and scarf over the hook by the door.

Too distracted to speak, it took him a moment to respond. "Um… Cornish hens and roasted fingerling potatoes."

"Sounds delicious! Will Fitz be joining us?"

The pup brought her a stuffed wool sock, wagging his tail in eager anticipation.

"A new toy?" She eyed it with an amused smile.

"It's a sock inside a sock," Jack explained, slipping on a pair of oven mitts. "He seems to like it. And I saved him some of the drippings to go with his dry food."

"Between the display and dog toys, you've become quite the crafter," she teased, tossing the sock for Fitz to fetch.

"What can I say? I'm a natural." As he slid the Cornish hens from the oven, he breathed a sigh of relief, admiring their perfectly golden sheen.

Truthfully, he couldn't wait to see their display all lit up the evening of the carnival. While it looked completed to the outside world—appeasing Mayor Burns—they'd decided to save the big reveal, setting a timer for the lights to turn on after nightfall on Christmas Day. He frequently daydreamed about witnessing the moment with Kat by his side... and maybe stealing a few moments beneath it.

"So, where are we going tonight?" No sooner than she'd seated herself at the table, Fitz pranced over, propping his head in her lap for more ear scratches.

Kat happily obliged, and Jack stole glances in their direction as he arranged the Cornish hens on a serving plate. He didn't think he could ever tire of the heart-melting sight.

"Do I have to explain how a surprise works?" Grinning, he set the plate beside the flickering candle.

He hoped he hadn't overdone it on the ambiance. Between the candlelight, crackling fire, and instrumental Christmas music playing softly in the background, the mood was decidedly romantic.

As he leaned across her to set the baking dish of garlic pota-toes in the last remaining inch of space, he caught a whiff of her perfume—heady with a hint of spice. He didn't recall smelling it before this evening.

His stomach performed a double backflip.

Was it possible he wasn't the only one with more than friend-ship in mind?

Or was it only wishful thinking?

❄

*K*at hadn't wanted dinner to end, but as they stood in the breathtaking cavern, she changed her mind, completely captivated by the stalactites dripping from the ceiling like a crystal chandelier above a stunning underground lake. The smooth-as-glass surface shimmered in the soft glow of several lanterns.

"Neat, huh?" Jack's arm brushed against hers in the dim lighting. And even though they both wore thick coats to ward against the cold, musty air inside the cave, the sensation spread a tingling warmth across her skin.

"It's the most beautiful sight I've ever seen."

"We'll have to come back in the summer when they hold concerts on the water. It's pretty incredible."

He'd said the words as casually as if he'd recited the weather report. Had he forgotten she'd be gone long before summertime? The thought immediately sobered her.

Their tour guide—a spry, elderly gentleman dressed like an eighteenth-century gold miner—raised his lantern, illuminating the dozen or so faces gazing at him in furtive anticipation. "Welcome to this year's Caroling in the Caves."

Kat's spine went rigid. More caroling? She'd barely made it through Pajama Christmas, her brain working overtime to suppress unwanted memories.

Jack reached for her hand, giving it a firm squeeze. "It's going to be great." His features softened as he smiled, and he looked so sweet and expectant, she couldn't argue.

Lacing her fingers through his, she squeezed back, relishing the comforting pressure of his palm against hers. It was the most intimate physical connection they'd ever shared, and she marveled at how safe and reassuring it felt. Maybe the experience wouldn't be so bad with Jack by her side.

A skilled soprano with a voice as high and impressive as the beehive of yellow curls pinned on top of her head led them in an a cappella rendition of "O Come, O Come, Emmanuel."

Kat merely listened at first, enchanted by the way their collective voices echoed throughout the cavern, so pure and ethereal it gave her chills.

And Jack? His rich, velvety baritone wrapped around her like a warm blanket, lulling her into such a serene state, she almost forgot where she was.

"I think we're coming up to the last few songs," he whispered, breaking her trance. "Why don't you give the next one a try?"

Although she hadn't sung a single note since her mother died, something in his earnest, hopeful expression provided the nudge she needed.

As the hauntingly beautiful melody of "I Wonder as I Wander" reverberated through the cavern, Kat closed her eyes, soaking it in.

The words escaped in a whisper at first, but as Jack tightened his grip, her confidence grew. When she found the harmony, their voices blended together, strong and soulful, as interwoven as their entwined fingers.

Losing herself in the transcendent sound, Kat found herself back at Hope Hideaway, snuggled in bed beside Helena while she sang her to sleep—the only time she'd ever felt her mother's love.

❄

*T*he hairs on Jack's arm stood on end as Kat's angelic voice washed over him. No, *angelic* didn't do it justice. She had the most beautiful voice he'd ever heard; he could listen for hours on end, soaking up every syllable.

And when they transitioned to their last song of the evening —a departure from the more traditional carols—Jack found himself leaning toward her, straining to catch every dulcet note.

But a few lines into "River" by Joni Mitchell, Kat's voice broke.

Glancing down, he noticed her cheeks glistened in the lantern light.

His stomach clenched. "Are you okay?"

She nodded, but the tears continued to tumble. Without a word, he tugged her hand, leading her back the way they'd entered.

Once outside, he turned to face her, gazing into her tear-filled eyes with concern. "What's wrong?"

"It's nothing." She sniffled, roughly wiping her damp cheek.

"Here, come with me." He led her down a narrow footpath to the Clearwater Cavern Visitors' Center. Beside the rustic, log-hewn structure, an event area boasting a roaring firepit, log benches, and picnic tables arranged with snacks and hot cider awaited the carolers.

After settling Kat on one of the benches, Jack filled two paper cups with piping-hot cider and carried them back to the firepit, sitting beside her. "When you're ready, I'm here to listen."

She gazed into the amber liquid as if studying the subtle wisps of steam curling into the frigid air. "That was my mother's favorite song," she said quietly. "Whenever I had a nightmare, she'd sing me to sleep. It was the only time she felt like—" She bit her bottom lip, as though afraid to continue.

He scooted closer on the log, silently offering his support.

Kat drew in a breath and slowly released it with her confession. "It was the only time she truly felt like a mother."

His heart wrenched. "I'm sorry I brought you here. I didn't realize—"

"Jack, I'm glad we came." She met his gaze with a soft smile. "It's silly, but I keep Helena's Joni Mitchell CD in my car, hidden beneath a bunch of papers in my glove compartment. It's like a part of me wants to remember the happy memories. But the other stronger part of me can't bear it."

She glanced at the flickering flames, the golden glow highlighting her wistful countenance. "Fern always says that love is generous. It chooses to see the good in people. But if I did that—looked for the good in my mother—I might have to let go of other things. Things I've clung to for most of my life. Honestly, the thought terrifies me."

Kat's vulnerability resonated with Jack on a deep, personal

level. There were things in his own life that had festered far too long.

But he wasn't sure what would happen if he tried to uproot them.

Or if he was even willing to find out.

CHAPTER 19

"*Y*ou're all set," Paul said in a wrapping-up tone. "But Jack, have you been out to the property recently?"

"Yeah, why?" Jack twirled a pen between his fingers, unconcerned.

"It's gone downhill over the years. It's going to take a lot of work to turn it into someplace inhabitable, let alone an inn with paying customers. Not to mention a ton of money." He paused before adding with a chuckle, "Not that you don't have plenty of that."

"Thanks for your concern, Paul. I'm willing to make the investment. It's a worthwhile project."

For more reasons than one....

As Jack hung up the phone, Vick ducked his head inside the office. "I thought you'd want to know Colt's mumbling something about truffle butter under his breath."

Jack shook his head in bemusement, in too good of a mood to be bothered by his friend's latest culinary ambitions. "Keep an eye on him. If he starts talking about importing truffles from France, let me know."

"Will do." Vick saluted before taking a step backward. Then, he hesitated in the doorway as if contemplating his next words. "Was that phone call about the Windsor place?"

The pen in Jack's hand stopped spinning. "How'd you hear about that?"

"It's a small town." Vick shrugged.

Jack knew that fact all too well, but his brooding, solitary cook usually kept to himself. If Vick knew about the inn, it was only a matter of time before Kat found out, too. And Jack wanted to be the one to tell her, but not until he'd made a little more progress.

"Don't worry," Vick told him. "I don't think your girlfriend knows anything about it."

Jack's lips quirked. Girlfriend, huh? Kat was hardly his girlfriend, but he didn't bother correcting him.

"I overheard a lady talking about it on the phone last night. She stopped by the diner looking for you. When Colt told her you were on a date, she stuck around for dinner. And dessert. I got the feeling she was waiting to see when you'd come back."

Jack suppressed a heavy sigh, knowing exactly who Vick was talking about. "Thanks for letting me know."

"About the Windsor place," Vick continued. "I have some experience with construction, if you need any help."

Now that Vick mentioned it, Jack remembered seeing something about that on his application when he'd hired him a few years ago. If he recalled, Vick had floated around from job to job after he got out of the military. "That's right. You worked for Camden Construction, right?"

"Yeah. It's a family-owned business. Great guys. I'm still friends with the son if you want a referral."

"You know what, that'd be great." The sooner he got started on renovations, the better. While he knew Luke would lend his woodworking skills and Reed would handle landscaping, he could use a professional construction crew.

"I'll give them a call," Vick offered. "Work is slow during the winter, so they may have some time."

"Perfect. Thanks."

Although Vick's muscular frame filled most of the narrow doorway, Colt managed to poke his head over his shoulder. "Ashley's here to see you." His tone complemented his eye roll.

Tossing his pen on the table, Jack stood with a grimace.

Both men gave him sympathetic glances as he squeezed past them.

Ashley waited near the entrance, her sleek, all-black outfit matching her somber expression.

"I heard you're looking for me," he said in a friendlier drawl than usual. Kat's words from last night had reminded him that he wouldn't get very far living in the past.

"I just wanted to say goodbye before I head back to LA."

Jack blinked, surprised by the news. "Okay, then. Hope you have a safe flight."

"Thanks." She turned toward the door, then glanced back. "Jack," she said tentatively.

He repressed a groan, worried she wanted to rehash old wounds again. But he stood his ground, resigned to let her speak her mind, then address whatever he needed to in order to help them both move on once and for all.

Her dark eyes softened. "I don't think you realize how much Lucy looks up to you. The very thought of disappointing... Well, let's just say it's not easy for her."

Taken aback, Jack didn't respond for several seconds. He hadn't expected Ashley to bring up Lucy, let alone with so much concern and affection. Finally, he cleared his throat. "I'll bear that in mind."

She offered a thin smile. "Merry Christmas, Jack."

"Merry Christmas, Tanner."

Her eyes widened, knowing full well that he only called friends by their last name.

This time, she flashed a broad, genuine smile before striding out the front door.

As he watched her go, Jack's chest expanded, as if letting go of his bitterness had suddenly made more room in his heart.

And he knew exactly how he wanted to fill it.

*a*s Kat's silver Toyota Corolla coasted along the scenic road leading into town, her heart felt light. Both because the picturesque view had become pleasantly familiar and because Fern's comforting voice crackled through her car's Bluetooth.

"I'm so happy you're enjoying yourself, mija," Fern said warmly. "Your sister sounds like a wonderful woman."

"She is," Kat said with complete sincerity. She didn't add that Penny had turned out to be nothing like their mother, as she'd feared. "I should have responded to her letter sooner."

She still hadn't told Fern about the brooch.

Or Jack.

"Well, you're there now. That's what matters. Have you met anyone else during your visit?"

Kat shifted her grip on the steering wheel, biding her time. "Um… a few. Friends of Penny, mostly. Some other guests at the inn." Before Fern could press further, Kat asked, "How is everyone at Hope Hideaway? I should be coming home soon. I miss you all." Although the words were true—she did miss them—her pulse stuttered at the thought of leaving Poppy Creek.

"We're doing just fine. A new woman joined us a few days ago. Ann. She's lovely. And a real wonder in the kitchen. Her second night, she made a big pot of the most delicious soup. Pho, I think she called it."

"That's wonderful," Kat told her, although her chest tightened. They were on the verge of closing and Fern was accepting new women into the shelter. Although arguably unwise, it wasn't all that surprising.

Fern seemed to read her mind. "Don't worry. It's the season for miracles, remember?"

"I remember." Her thoughts drifted to the brooch. She needed to focus, not fritter away her time with hopeless fantasies about a certain restaurant owner. Fern was counting on her.

She pulled into a parking spot a few spaces down from Thistle & Thorn and shut off the engine.

"It was good to hear your voice," Fern said, sensing she'd come to a stop. "But don't you worry about us. We're doing just fine. Enjoy getting to know your sister. And anyone else of interest."

Kat couldn't help a smile at her subtle insinuation. "I will."

After she exited the car, she paused a moment, taking in the town square. Most of the storefront displays were nearing completion and the entire town looked as festive as the North Pole. Her gaze rested on Jack's diner and their mistletoe-covered arbor. While still beautiful in daylight, with its dripping greenery and red ribbons and bows, she knew it would look stunning at night, illuminated with hundreds of twinkling lights. And she couldn't wait to see it.

She couldn't wait to see Jack, either. But she needed to push those thoughts from her mind. If she wasn't careful, spending time with Jack would preempt all other priorities.

As she neared the entrance to Thistle & Thorn, Kat admired Penny's display. Her sister and her fiancé had arranged the front of the store to look like Santa's workshop, but all the toys were vintage, gifting passersby with a nostalgic glimpse into their childhood.

"How was your date?" Penny asked eagerly the second Kat crossed the threshold.

"I don't think it was a date, per se…." Her cheeks heated.

"Oh, it was definitely a date. Colt said Jack took you caroling at Clearwater Cavern. How was it?"

"It was breathtaking. I've never seen—or heard—anything so beautiful."

Penny's eyes took on a dreamy glaze. "It's one of my favorite spots in the whole world. Colt took me to a classical concert inside the cavern last summer. In fact, it's where we had our first kiss."

For a brief moment, Kat wished she could say the same about her and Jack. But while there hadn't been a kiss, she had felt closer to Jack after sharing more about her past. Their connection seemed to be growing all the time. But to what end? He couldn't leave Poppy Creek and his thriving business. And she could never leave Fern and Hope Hideaway. They were doomed to part from the very beginning.

"You and Colt seem really happy together," she said wistfully.

"We are. Although, don't get me wrong, things aren't always easy. We have our share of squabbles and obstacles. But when you find that person who makes it all worth it..." Her features settled in a blissful smile before she added wryly, "Now, if we could only figure out the wedding."

"What are your plans so far?"

"None, really. We can't decide when or where we want it. Or what style, what colors—anything." She threw up her hands in exasperation.

"There's nothing you like?"

"The opposite, actually. I have too many ideas and I can't decide. While poor Colt doesn't care about all the details. He just wants to get married as soon as possible."

"That's sweet." Kat smiled. "Well, I'm sure, in time, everything will come together perfectly."

"Thank you. I'm sure you're right. And I hope, whenever we wind up getting married, that you'll be there."

"I wouldn't miss it."

"Excellent." Penny grinned, although her eyes glistened with emotion. Providing some levity, she asked, "Are you ready for the next clue? It's a doozy."

"Ready." Kat joined her at the old-fashioned checkout counter as Penny retrieved the slip of paper from the pocket of her 1930s-style tweed suit.

"'North, south, east, west, they stretch from sea to sea. But which direction is the best? It's always number three.'" Penny glanced up. "I thought maybe it could be referring to the globe in my dad's room. Or his collection of old nautical charts. Or perhaps the map of the world hanging in the living room. I briefly checked all three, but couldn't find anything. I'm hoping you'll have more luck."

"Me, too," Kat agreed, though the words tasted bittersweet.

Once she found the brooch, she'd have to leave a whole lot more behind.

CHAPTER 20

Standing shoulder to shoulder with Luke, Vick, and Reed, Jack scrutinized the Windsor house and the enormity of the project that lay before him.

Vick whistled. "It's in worse shape than I thought." As soon as the words left his lips, a hinge creaked in the wind. Coming loose, the decrepit shutter flopped to the side, dangling by the one hinge it had left.

Jack winced.

"The property isn't much better," Reed noted, surveying the barren landscape. Weeds appeared to be the only thriving foliage.

"I think it's great." Luke placed a reassuring hand on his shoulder. "I wish I'd thought of buying Cassie an inn last Christmas when I was trying to convince her to stay in Poppy Creek."

"I think it worked out okay, even without the inn," Reed said with a grin.

"True." Luke chuckled. "And the coffee shop is more her style, anyway."

Fitz trotted over from the neighboring trees and dropped a stick at Jack's feet. Kneeling down, Jack rubbed the dog's head.

Being back in the spot where they'd found the pup stirred Jack's sentimental side.

"How does he get along with Grant's dog?" Reed bent down to run a hand over his soft fur.

"They actually haven't met yet. Vinny stays at Eliza's place. But we hope to get them together soon." Secretly, the idea of a double date with the dogs thrilled Jack. And he fantasized about life with Kat more often than he should.

While he hoped the inn would entice her to stay, it wasn't his only reason for renovating the house. Being around Kat had made him realize how selfish and shortsighted he'd been letting the property go to waste. And whether or not she stayed, she'd inspired him to do more with his money and possessions.

Rising to his feet, stick in hand, Jack threw it into the tree line, smiling as Fitz bounded after it.

At the sound of tires crunching over gravel, all four men turned toward the approaching vehicle.

A large diesel pickup truck with Camden Construction emblazoned on the side rolled to a stop. A trim man in his early sixties climbed out of the driver's seat, his sun-worn skin and fit frame hinting at his line of work.

A younger version of the man hopped out of the passenger side, his sturdy work boots and substantial build making a sizable imprint in the loose gravel. "Hey, Vick. Long time no see."

The two men exchanged a side-hug greeting before slapping each other on the back and grinning broadly.

Although they couldn't have looked more different—Vick was edgy and tattooed while his friend had a more wholesome, boy-next-door appearance—they were clearly good friends.

"Jack Gardener?" the older man asked, searching their faces.

Jack stepped forward and extended his hand. "That's me."

"Tom Camden. And this is my son, Noah."

"I appreciate you guys coming out here on such short notice."

"No problem. Business slows down in the winter. There isn't

a lot we can do in the rain or snow. But we can take a look at the place and get started on what we can, weather permitting. What kind of a time frame are we looking at?"

"The sooner the better, but I'm flexible."

"Great. Let's take a look at what we're working with." Placing a hand on his son's shoulder, he said, "You and Vick check out the exterior, paying close attention to the roof. I'll have Jack show me around inside."

"You got it, Pops." Noah flashed his father an affable grin, highlighting their easygoing relationship.

The contrast to Jack's relationship with his own father wasn't lost on him, and his footsteps felt heavy as he led the way inside.

Although the bones of the structure were solid, the interior damage was fairly extensive. As he showed Tom the deteriorating fixtures and crumbling walls, he asked, "Is the business just you and your son?"

"We have a crew of half a dozen guys. But my son is my right-hand man. I taught him everything I know. And I plan to pass him the reins when I'm ready to retire."

Jack's stomach clenched at the note of pride in Tom's voice.

"I don't think anything can make a father prouder than when his son wants to follow in his footsteps. When my eldest son told me he wanted to open a health food store, it was a hard pill to swallow."

The knot in Jack's stomach tightened.

"You have kids?" Tom asked.

"No, I don't." Although, he'd been thinking about the prospect of having a family more often these days.

"Ah well, it's easier to understand when you have kids of your own. But as a parent, it can be difficult to separate wanting what's best for your kids with your own ego. It took me a while to figure that out. Rather, it took me a while to listen to my wife." He chuckled as he turned on the kitchen faucet.

Nothing happened.

Either the water had been shut off or the pipes were frozen, Jack wasn't sure. But Tom didn't seem overly concerned.

"I'm just glad my son was able to forgive my bullheadedness," he continued good-naturedly, unaware of how his words affected his companion.

Clearing his throat, Jack nodded toward the rusty fixture. "Do you think it's beyond repair?"

Tom smiled. "One thing you learn in my line of work… if it's important enough, you'll find a way to fix it."

For a fleeting moment, Jack wondered if he meant far more than the faucet.

❄

*K*at and Penny had searched the globe and nautical charts to no avail.

Chip had even tried to help by chewing off a corner of one of the charts.

Kat had stifled her laughter as Penny wrangled the scrap of paper from his mouth.

Last but not least, they'd moved on to the map in a large ornate frame—the impressive, hand-carved kind Kat suspected should be in a museum encasing a Rembrandt painting.

Taking each side, they carefully lifted it off the wall and flipped it over, checking the backing for a tear or incision indicating there could be something hidden inside the canvas.

While they combed every inch, Penny said in an offhand manner, "I heard Ashley left town today."

"Oh?" Kat's heartbeat skipped, but she managed to keep her expression aloof.

"Apparently, she came by the diner last night looking for Jack, and Colt told her he was on a date with you."

Feeling her cheeks flush, Kat kept her head down, focused on their task.

"He said that for the rest of the evening, she sat at a booth facing the front door, ordering gobs of food while working on her laptop until closing."

Kat didn't have to guess why, assuming she'd been waiting to see when Jack returned. If she were in the other woman's shoes, she might have been tempted to do the same thing. "Do you think she wants Jack back?"

"It appears that way. But besides the fact that she left town after high school and never spoke to Jack or any of her friends ever again, Jack's affections seem to be elsewhere."

Kat's blush deepened.

Penny paused her search, gazing at Kat with gentle concern. "Jack was pretty devastated when Ashley left. I'd hate to see that happen again."

Kat sobered, realizing the weight of her sister's words.

"So would I," she murmured softly. "But no matter how badly I want things to work out, I don't see how they can. His life is here, and mine…" Her voice fell away.

Over the last several days, she'd had a niggling feeling that her life in Starcross Cove was only a shadow of what it could be. Or perhaps more accurately, a shadow of someone else's.

"I know," Penny agreed mournfully. "And I wish I had a helpful answer. But I choose to believe a miracle can happen that will allow you two to be together."

Kat smiled, tears stinging her eyes. Her sister sounded so much like Fern in that moment.

Sniffling, she said, "We're going to need a couple of miracles. Because I don't think the brooch is in here." With a sigh, she leaned the frame against the wall.

Penny took a step back, studying it with a contemplative squint. "I feel like we're missing something. Can you read the clue again?"

Kat plucked the slip of paper from the side table. "'North, south, east, west, they stretch from sea to sea. But which direction is the best? It's always number three.'" For some reason, this time, the last line stood out to her. "Three... three..." She tapped her fingertip against her lips in thought. After a moment, an idea struck her. "Three!"

"What?" Penny asked. "What did you figure out?"

"It's the line that says 'the best is number three.'" Running her finger along the paper, she landed on east—the third direction listed. "Check the east side of the frame. For a nick or groove or anything out of the ordinary."

After Penny searched for a few minutes, she frowned. "I can't find anything. But it's hard to tell with the intricate engraving." Suddenly, her eyes widened. "Wait!" She removed an antique hair comb from her elegant updo and bent one of the prongs. Squinting, she inserted the tip into a tiny hole, and a small section of the frame popped open.

"You've got to be kidding," Kat breathed, completely amazed.

"I should have thought of this sooner. Dad's campaign desk has a secret compartment, too." Penny wriggled the drawer out a little farther, revealing another note.

The girls exchanged glances.

"I love my dad, but even I'm getting a little exhausted," Penny admitted with a shaky smile.

"He definitely seems to have gotten carried away. But I imagine he planned on doing the treasure hunt with you, helping when needed."

"That's true." Her smile broadened, encouraged by the thought.

"What does it say?" Kat asked.

"'The seven seas I used to sail, the sky was once my stage. But the greatest story I'll regale, belongs upon the page.'"

"Hmm. Is it just me, or do they keep getting harder?" Suddenly drained, she sank onto the brocade settee by the window. "Maybe there are easier ways to raise money for Hope Hideaway. Like winning the lottery." She grinned ruefully.

Penny laughed. "I know I've said this before, but I'm glad your visit keeps getting extended. In fact, there's somewhere I'd like you to go with me tonight."

"Where?"

"The library."

"The library?" Kat echoed in confusion. Why would they be going to the library in the evening? Wouldn't it be closed?

"Yep," Penny said brightly. "But first, we have to find you something to wear."

Kat glanced down at her jeans and cable-knit sweater—simple and timeless. Certainly suitable attire for the library.

What exactly did Penny have in mind?

CHAPTER 21

As they approached the library, Kat's breath caught in her throat. The historic brick building with its stately white columns would be considered eye-catching on any occasion, but tonight, with votive candles lining the stone steps and greenery arched above the double doors, it looked enchanting.

"Madam," Colt drawled in a cheesy British accent, offering Kat the crook of his elbow.

Clinging to his other arm, Penny smirked in amusement before mentioning, "The stone steps get a little icy at night."

Kat gratefully accepted the offer, not wanting to risk breaking an ankle in her three-inch heels.

Not for the first time that evening, she wondered if Jack would be there. Although it seemed silly, she hoped he would get to see her all dressed up. The floor-length vintage gown in the softest red velvet fit her frame as though it had been tailor-made to suit her exact measurements. And Penny had managed to tame her wild mane into silky waves that cascaded around her shoulders.

A rush of warm air collided with the evening chill as they crossed the threshold into the lobby. More votive candles guided them toward the back room, which housed first editions and special hardback collections. It was by far the most impressive space in the entire library, with its ornate marble fireplace, tall bay windows, and crystal chandelier.

Tonight, two people would be joined together in marriage before a few dozen of their closest friends and family. And Kat still couldn't believe she got to be a part of the magical evening.

As they entered the room, soft, romantic lighting and soothing classical music greeted them.

Wooden folding chairs faced the marble fireplace, arranged to create an aisle down the middle. There were no wedding decorations to speak of, but they were hardly needed. The room itself, composed of polished mahogany shelves filled with the most exquisitely bound books, boasted enough beauty on its own.

Slipping out of her kelly-green coat, she draped it over one arm, sensing all eyes turn on her as they moved down the rows of folding chairs.

She smiled, recognizing the couple from the inn, and returned their friendly wave.

But one gaze in particular made her heart stand still.

The affection and admiration in Jack's eyes couldn't be missed, and his glance was at once smoldering and scintillatingly sweet.

Her skin tingled all the way to her toes, and she nearly tripped over the ivory aisle runner.

"We're in that row, up there," Penny whispered, pointing to where Jack sat, drinking her in with his gaze.

Her throat went dry. She'd have to sit beside him for the entire ceremony? How would she concentrate?

She curled her fingers into her palm, recalling the sensation of his hand wrapped around hers the night they went caroling. There was something so life-giving in his touch. It made her feel like anything was possible.

Even a miracle.

❄

*I*f Jack hadn't already been sitting down, he would have toppled over at the sight of Kat.

Her dress clung to every curve with an effortless ease he found unbelievably distracting. And her fiery red hair shimmered in the subdued lighting, tempting him to run his fingers through the silky waves.

Heat crept up his neck and he shook the thoughts aside as she slid onto the seat beside him, followed by Penny and Colt.

"Hi," she murmured, her lips curled into a shy smile.

"Hi," he croaked in return. He still couldn't believe she was there, sitting next to him. He'd longed to invite her but also wanted to respect Frank and Beverly's request to keep the gathering small and intimate, since neither one enjoyed the spotlight. But he should've known she'd come with Penny. And he couldn't be happier about it.

"You look…" he began hoarsely, but words failed him.

"Thank you." Her cheeks flushed a pretty pink tinge. "So do you."

"You mean, this old thing?" He flashed a rueful grin, running a hand down the lapel of his navy suit. Lucy had bought it for him, claiming the color enhanced the blue of his eyes. Of course, he didn't care about that, but he did appreciate that the material was buttery smooth and he could move his arms without feeling like they were encased in cardboard.

Her smile broadened, as though his playful humor set her at ease. At least, he liked to think that was the reason. But what would calm his racing heartbeat? At any moment, it was bound to burst right out of his rib cage.

Sitting so close to her in such a romantic setting while not being about to drape his arm around her shoulders or lace his fingers through hers would be akin to torture.

All throughout the ceremony, his attention wandered to

daydreams of him and Kat standing in Frank and Beverly's place one day. Perhaps it was the ambiance or the surge of emotions, but as he watched two people he cared deeply about proclaim their love for one another, the idea of marriage seemed more and more appealing—and increasingly possible.

But as the vision of their wedding played out in his mind, he was struck by a sobering realization. He couldn't imagine a ceremony without his family present—*all* of his family.

He pushed the thought aside, trying to focus on Frank and Beverly as they joined hands, ready to exchange their vows.

Frank—dapper in a charcoal-gray wool suit and Sinatra-inspired fedora—cleared his throat, his nerves evident by the visible tremor in his fingers.

"I'm not one for fancy words," he began, his voice gravelly. "Or maybe it's like that Mr. Knightly says in your favorite book, 'If I loved you less, I might be able to talk about it more.'"

At that, Beverly smiled, touched by the quote from Jane Austen's *Emma*.

"Either way," he continued, "it's difficult to explain how I went from being a crotchety old Scrooge who'd run out of hope to the happiest man alive, getting married right before Christmas. I guess miracles really do happen."

Everyone chuckled, and Frank's nerves seemed to settle. "I can't promise I'll never grumble again or sneak a cup of regular coffee when I'm supposed to have decaf. And I may still fall asleep at the end of every *Columbo* episode and ask you how he solved the crime."

More snickers, and this time, Beverly joined in, her sweet, lilting laugh rising above the rest.

"But I can promise," Frank added with conviction, "that I'll love you more the next day than the one before. And whenever you count your wrinkles and gray hairs, lamenting your lost youth, I'll remind you that Grace Kelly in her prime couldn't hold a candle to your beauty, even now."

Beverly blushed beneath his ardent gaze, and as Jack considered the two lovebirds, each well beyond his years, he didn't doubt Frank believed every word.

In Frank's eyes, his bride—dressed in a simple yet elegant ivory dress, her dove-white hair twisted on top of her head—was the most beautiful woman in existence.

Jack stole a sideways glance at Kat, admiring each graceful line of her profile. He could relate to Frank's sentiments because he had never glimpsed a more stunning woman, inside and out.

She'd captured his heart with her compassion and kindness—qualities that far surpassed any physical characteristic, although her beauty was unparalleled. And as he sat beside her, the intimacy of the moment provided such startling clarity, he couldn't deny the truth even if he'd wanted to.

He loved Kat Bennet.

The kind of love that stirred his soul and inspired him to be a better man.

He stole another glance in her direction, this time catching her eye. The heat from her gaze seared through his skin and he almost lost himself in the moment when Frank cleared his throat again.

"When all is said and done," Frank said, his voice thick and husky, "you might be getting the raw end of this deal. But what do you say, Bevy? Will you be my wife 'til we're seated at the big coffee shop in the sky?"

"With all my heart, yes," she murmured, her pale blue eyes glistening. "I knew the moment we first met at last year's Christmas Eve dance that you were someone special, Frank Barrie. Right away, I could tell you were as sweet as a Cadbury egg. You may have had a hard outer shell, but you were soft on the inside."

This time, Frank flushed, but more pleased than embarrassed.

"I was a widow for so long, I never expected to find this kind of love again. Once is a blessing. But twice? I didn't dare hope.

And yet, standing here today, at the grand old age of—" She paused. "Well, not nineteen."

Soft laughter sprinkled around the room.

"You make me feel like a blushing bride again—young and carefree, but also safe and deeply known. That kind of love is worth holding on to, no matter the obstacles."

Jack felt Kat shift by his side. She stared into her lap, blinking hard. He would have given anything to know what she was thinking at that moment.

"We've had a bumpy road getting here, but I would do it all again, a million times over, if it meant being your wife until the Lord brings us home."

As Beverly concluded her vows, and Pastor Bellman pronounced them husband and wife, the room erupted in cheers and applause as the newlyweds kissed.

They exited to "You Make Me Feel So Young" by Frank Sinatra, leading the guests into the lobby of the library for the simple hors d'oeuvre reception.

Kat stood, preparing to follow Penny and Colt, but Jack gently grabbed her elbow.

Her eyes wide and questioning, she turned to face him.

Suddenly nervous, he gathered a breath. "I was wondering... how do you feel about wassailing?"

*a*s she sat in the passenger seat of Jack's truck, Kat wrapped a loose thread from her scarf around her pinky. In her dazed state, she coiled it so tightly, she cut off the circulation, turning the tip white.

Jack cast a worried side-glance in her direction. "Are you okay?"

"Uh-huh," she lied, unraveling the strand to restore blood flow to her throbbing finger.

"If it makes you feel any better, I'm nervous, too," he admitted, turning onto State Street. "And it means a lot to me that you're here."

He gifted her with a warm, grateful smile that momentarily eased her frantic nerves.

Focusing her gaze on the twinkling lights creating a canopy above the tree-lined street, she tried to settle her racing heart by taking slow, intentional breaths.

When Jack had explained his family's wassailing tradition and invited her to join them, she'd been touched and surprised. Considering his long-standing feud with his father, she hadn't expected Jack to go home during the holidays, let alone request her company.

On one hand, she couldn't help reading into the significance of his invitation. It had to mean something. One didn't simply bring a casual acquaintance along for such a monumental occasion, did they?

On the other hand, she wasn't convinced meeting his family under such tense circumstances was a good idea. Maybe he should break the ice with his father first?

As if reading her thoughts, Jack added, "Don't worry. My family takes hosting very seriously. In their mind, a tense or uncomfortable moment is as unforgivable as serving lukewarm tea to the Queen of England."

Despite her anxious energy, Kat smiled. "And you're sure they won't mind me coming along?"

"Mind? They'll be thrilled. Especially Lucy. She squealed on the phone for five whole minutes when I told her we'd be coming. I thought for sure she would pass out from lack of oxygen."

Kat's hands relaxed in her lap, comforted by the thought of finally meeting Jack's sister. The woman sounded as warm and kindhearted as Jack, and she had a feeling they'd be fast friends. At least, she hoped they would be.

"Jack…" She hesitated, wanting to tread carefully. "Do you think it would be helpful if I knew what happened between you and your father? I wonder if having some context or background would help me interpret the dynamics between the two of you."

He shifted his grip on the steering wheel, contemplating her question. When they reached the end of State Street, he turned right onto a wide, scenic road. The large, luxurious homes on either side seemed to increase in grandeur as they rumbled past.

"I want to tell you everything," Jack said, sounding sincere. "But we're almost there. For now, let's just say my father used his wealth and connections to influence my life in a less than positive way. And he knew exactly what he was doing."

Kat nodded, her chest aching on his behalf. While her emotions toward her mother were complicated—and Helena had caused her enough pain to last two lifetimes—her wounds were indirect consequences of her mother's vices, not intentionally inflicted as Jack's had been. Not that the knowledge made it any easier to forgive her.

"I'm sorry," she murmured, subconsciously resting her hand on the bench seat between them.

She hadn't realized she'd done so until he reached for her, entwining their fingers as he steered with one hand. He paired a gentle squeeze with another smile that made her heart flutter. "I know I've said this before, but I really appreciate you being here." He looked like he was about to say more, but they'd arrived at their destination. Releasing her hand, he put his truck in park.

A pang of disappointment rippled through her, but when she glanced up, her shock took over.

The palatial Georgian-style mansion seemed to stretch on forever, ending in a carriage house that had been modified into a massive garage that could easily fit a fleet of fancy cars.

A department-store-worthy tree stood in the center of the circular driveway and a coordinating wreath hung on each window and door, of which there were several. Every light in the home appeared to be switched on, and coupled with the lampposts lining the drive, the entire house glowed against the backdrop of the wintry night sky.

No sooner than he'd flicked off the headlights, the front door swung open and a young woman emerged in full Victorian garb. Her pristine updo—glossy, period-appropriate ringlets that framed her pretty face—threatened to come loose as she skipped down the stone steps and raced across the gravel drive.

"That's Lucy," Jack chuckled as he hopped out of the driver's seat. "Get ready to be hugged."

Kat watched, unable to hide a smile as Lucy tackled Jack in a bone-crushing hug, rumpling her elegant dress in the process.

"Easy," Jack gasped. "I won't be able to sing if you collapse my lungs."

"Good," she giggled. "Then Liam will owe me one. He's always complaining you sing over him, since you're the only two baritones in the family." Noticing Kat, Lucy beamed in her direction. "You must be Kat, who I've heard so much about."

Without hesitation, Lucy gathered Kat in a welcoming hug, thankfully using less force than she had on her brother. "I'm so glad you could come. Mom and I are sorely outnumbered by the boys. And Jack said you have the voice of an angel."

Kat flushed, stealing a glance at Jack. His complexion appeared particularly rosy, but she reasoned it could be from the cold.

He cleared his throat. "Are you going to invite us inside? Or should we freeze out here in the driveway?"

Rolling her eyes, Lucy tucked her arm through Kat's, leading her toward the house. "I don't know how you put up with my brother."

"I think it's his cooking," Kat teased. "He makes the best flapjacks."

Jack caught her eye and the look that passed between them set her cheeks ablaze.

And in that moment, she had a feeling the night would be nothing short of perfect.

*W*hen Lucy whisked Kat away after introductions to change into her caroling costume, Jack felt oddly exposed. Her presence had provided a buffer, and now, standing in the middle of the opulent sitting room, his collar dug into his throat. He tugged, but it hardly budged.

"She's lovely, Jack." His mother broke the awkward silence as she flitted toward the rolling drink cart to top off her eggnog.

Elaine Gardener hadn't aged a day since Jack last saw his mother. Her pale-blond hair remained coiled in a permanent bun. And if anything, her porcelain skin had fewer wrinkles than he remembered.

"She's pretty great," he said flatly, not ready to divulge the full extent of his feelings.

"How'd you trick her into dating you?" Liam, his youngest brother, teased from his lounging position in the overstuffed armchair by the fire. He looked so grown up in his elaborate ensemble that included white gloves and a top hat.

"Did she ever eat at your diner?" Everett asked with a devilish grin. "I'm going to bet on food poisoning. It can make people delirious." As the middle child, his jokes were always a tad over the top.

"That's certainly a possibility," Jack chuckled. He'd missed their good-natured ribbing. And truthfully, he regretted letting the bad blood with his father come between him and his brothers. He should've made more of an effort to stay in touch.

"Don't listen to them." Micah, the second oldest, rested a hand on Jack's shoulder. "They're just bitter because you've found yourself a woman like Kat and we're all still single."

"It's a travesty," Elaine announced. "All my boys are tall, handsome, and successful. What's not to love?" She cupped Emmett's cheek, gazing at him fondly.

Jack was glad to see Emmett had finally differentiated himself from Everett with a closely trimmed beard. As identical twins, they had always been difficult for Jack to tell apart. Which they used to pull numerous pranks in their childhood.

"Successful to varying degrees." Richard Gardener poured bourbon from a Waterford crystal decanter into a matching tumbler.

Jack gritted his teeth, suspecting the clarification was meant for his benefit. Maybe a holiday truce had been expecting too much.

Micah cleared his throat. "Ready to don your fancy duds? Lucy rented all the costumes from some production company that specializes in Victorian-era films. Since you're the eldest, your outfit comes with a cane." He flashed a wry grin.

"Hilarious," Jack snorted, grateful to his brother for lightening the mood.

He'd known coming tonight wouldn't be easy. But if he could swallow his pride, he had a slim chance of getting through the rest of the evening without his temper flaring.

Being back among his family, he realized he didn't want to lose them again.

And not even his father's underhanded remarks could ruin the joyful occasion.

At least, not if he could help it.

$\mathcal{A}$s Kat stared at her reflection in the spotless bathroom mirror, she hardly recognized herself. In fact, in her gorgeous blue silk gown, she could have been mistaken for a character in Louisa May Alcott's *Little Women*.

Her gaze drifted to the nearby Chippendale chair where a coordinating blue cape and luxurious muff waited to complete her extravagant ensemble.

Extravagant was how she'd come to describe everything in the Gardener household, particularly the guest bathroom that boasted a porcelain claw-foot tub, endless marble countertops, and plush hand towels she'd been too afraid to touch. Instead, she'd dried her hands on her wool sweater.

"I love your hair. It's so rare to see this color red." Lucy stood behind her, pinning the last remaining strands in place. When she'd finished, she reached for the hot curling iron.

"Thanks." Kat straightened, trying to sit as still as possible on the stiff, embroidered stool. "I never liked my hair growing up. I was teased a lot."

"I'm sorry. Kids can be so cruel. That's why I'm glad I grew up with brothers. Once, a boy teased me about the gap between my front teeth, and Jack threatened to feed him a face full of dirt for lunch." She laughed as she checked the temperature of the wand by sprinkling a drop of water from the gilded faucet.

The ceramic cylinder sizzled as steam wafted into the air.

"Perfect." Lucy lifted a face-framing tendril and wrapped it around the barrel.

Although curly, Kat's wild mane was far from symmetrical ringlets.

"I love how close the two of you are," Kat told her, making conversation as she kept her spine rigid and tried not to think about the intense heat so close to her sensitive skin.

Lucy smiled, though somewhat wistfully. "We used to be closer. The hostility between Jack and our dad has taken a toll on all of us, to be honest. Although, I can't say I blame Jack. What our father did to him was pretty terrible."

Kat stared blankly, and Lucy's expressive blue eyes widened. "He didn't tell you, did he?"

"No. At least, not all the details," Kat admitted.

Lucy sighed as she coiled another strand of hair around the curling wand. "He's not very good at talking about his feelings, is he? You know, I don't even think he talked to dad about what happened. And of course, he would never say a word to me about it. Like a typical big brother, he's tried to shield me from things my entire life."

"If you don't mind me asking, how did you find out about it?"

"Ashley told me, if you can believe it. That's how I knew she wasn't right for my brother. She didn't see anything wrong with the situation."

Kat folded her hands in her lap and bit her bottom lip. She wouldn't pry. Jack would tell her when he was ready.

"Of course, there were other reasons I'm glad they didn't work out," Lucy continued. "With Ashley, it was purely infatuation. The kind of puppy love where you see the person for who you want them to be, not who they really are. But when Jack called and told me about you..." As she met Kat's gaze in the mirror, a grin spread across her face. "With you, I can tell it's the real deal."

Heat swept across Kat's cheeks, and this time, it wasn't from the curling iron.

Would tonight be the night Jack would finally confess his feelings for her?

※

To Jack's relief, the remainder of the evening unfolded without incident.

In fact, everyone seemed to be having a terrific time, including Kat.

Since Lucy and their mother were sopranos, everyone raved about the addition of Kat's contralto range, claiming she finally rounded out the troupe.

Lucy, in particular, seemed to thrive with another girl around. And nothing filled Jack's heart with more joy than witnessing his two favorite women getting along so well.

After caroling, they returned home, changed out of their costumes, and enjoyed a delicious five-course meal. While Jack would have preferred something simple and classic rather than a dish he couldn't even pronounce, he had to give credit to the chef; everything tasted exceptional.

To wrap up the evening, they retired to the sitting room for games and an assortment of festive desserts paired with mulled wine.

When Kat excused herself to use the restroom after a lively round of Pictionary, Liam asked, "When are you going to seal the deal with Kat? Because if you don't ask her to marry you, I might."

Jack laughed, helping himself to another serving of peanut brittle.

"Do you really think she'd go out with you once she knows I'm an option?" Emmett goaded his younger brother.

"You'd all better be quiet," Lucy scolded. "Do you want Kat to come back and hear you fools fighting over her?"

"Why not?" Everett grinned. "Perhaps we should duel for her hand in marriage like in grand old Victorian England."

"Good grief." Lucy rolled her eyes. "Clearly those costumes I rented have gone to your heads."

"What do you say, old chap?" Everett turned to Jack, tipping an imaginary top hat. "Are you prepared to fight for your lady's hand?"

"You haven't been able to beat me in a skirmish yet," Jack challenged. Although all of his brothers stood over six feet tall, he had a good inch or two on Everett.

"Aye. But I was but a wee lad back then. And ye didn't fight fair."

"Are you supposed to be British or Irish?" Micah asked, watching the amusing exchange from his corner of the couch.

"He sounds like a pirate to me," Liam snorted over the rim of his glass.

"Dad, can't you make them behave?" Lucy pleaded. "They're going to embarrass me in front of Kat."

"Speaking of Kat..." Emmett glanced toward the hallway. "She's been gone awhile."

"Ladies take their time in the powder room," Everett told him with a superior smirk. "You'd know that if you ever had a girlfriend."

Emmett threatened to toss a throw pillow at his twin, but reconsidered when he caught their mother's stern glare.

"Maybe she got lost," Micah offered helpfully. "With all the rooms and hallways, this house is like a maze."

"I'll go look." Lucy sprang from the couch, but Jack set his drink on the coffee table.

"No, I'll go. You try to get these hooligans under control while I'm gone."

"I'll do my best." She sighed heavily, as though she didn't have high hopes for her success.

Jack bit back another chuckle as he walked into the hall, over-hearing his brothers argue over which one of them was Kat's type.

Philistines, every single one of them. But he loved them anyway. And boy, did it feel good to be reunited with his family again.

Eventually, he'd have to confront his father about the past.

But for now, he'd savor the present.

And look forward to the future.

CHAPTER 24

*J*ack found her in the den, which was basically a carbon copy of the sitting room but with different decor.

For a moment, he stood in the doorway, not making a sound. She looked so beautiful gazing at the Christmas tree, framed by the frosted bay window. The glittering lights cast a colorful glow across her features as she admired the ornaments.

He held his breath, wanting to drink in the sight for as long as possible. But as he shifted his feet, the floorboards creaked beneath his weight.

Startled, she glanced up. The instant she met his gaze, a slow smile spread across her face, sending his pulse into overdrive.

"I was starting to worry you'd found the wardrobe that leads to another land," he teased, moving toward her.

"I did get a little bit lost, but then I found this tree..." She gently grazed a star crafted out of dry macaroni. "It's so different from the others."

Jack took a step closer. Now that she mentioned it, all of the other trees in the house—and there were several—appeared professionally decorated with distinct color schemes and

152

matching baubles. However, this one boasted a hodgepodge of handmade ornaments.

He peered closer, his eyes widening as they rested on the nativity set Everett made in first grade. He'd glued pieces of Lego to a strip of cardboard, using a T. rex instead of a donkey and Darth Vader as Joseph.

The angel Lucy had made by attaching construction paper wings to her Barbie hung a few branches higher. Jack's throat tightened. He'd assumed they'd all been thrown away. To find them here, adorning a tree where anyone could see them... he wasn't sure what to think.

"This one made me laugh." Kat drew his attention to a smooth round stone with a string tied around its middle. Although hanging from a sturdy branch, the bough bent beneath the weight.

"Look what it says." Grinning, she lifted a tag secured to the string. The sloppy handwriting read *Nutcracker*.

Jack returned her smile, recalling the exact evening he'd made the ornament. At nine years old, he'd felt pretty clever. "When you don't have money for decorations, you get creative."

"I love it," she announced with conviction. "All of it. This is the most incredible Christmas tree I've ever seen."

Jack had to agree. Unexpectedly overcome with emotion, he murmured, "Thank you."

"For what?" She turned to face him. She stood so close he could smell her heady perfume mingled with the scent of pine.

"For coming with me tonight. I don't know if I would have had the courage to come on my own."

"You would have," she said softly, "but I'm glad I came."

"Why did you?" His question escaped the back of his throat in a low, gravelly breath.

"What do you mean?" She seemed surprised by his question.

"Why did you agree to come with me?" he repeated, speaking without forethought. Suddenly, he desperately needed answers to all the uncertainty between them. "I know why I invited you. In the short amount of time that we've known each other, you've become one of the most important people in my life. And I can't really explain it, except to say…" He reached for her hands, relishing how soft yet strong they felt in his grasp. "I'm falling in love with you, Kat. And I'm wondering if there's even a small chance you might feel the same way."

A pleasant shiver skittered down Kat's spine as Jack said her name in a hoarse whisper.

Before, he'd always used her last name, which she'd learned was a sign of friendship. But the way he'd said *Kat*—so fervent and heartfelt—she lost all control of her senses.

Stretching onto her tiptoes, she slid her arms around his neck.

Their lips met with a startling sense of urgency, and yet, his kiss held such intoxicating tenderness. She had no idea how long they stood there, immersed in the moment, entranced by the exhilarating feel of being so close to each other.

A throat cleared, severing their connection like scissors snipping a thread.

They quickly broke apart, creating physical distance, although the euphoric haze lingered.

Lucy hid a smirk. "Mom wants to start our Christmas Wish tradition. Should I tell them you two are busy?"

Kat's entire face blazed as Jack blurted, "We're coming."

Lucy's gaze traveled above their heads, her grin growing wider. "Mistletoe strikes again, I see. The sneaky sprig."

Confused, Kat glanced up. Sure enough, a green sprig dotted with white berries dangled from the center of the chandelier.

Jack released a low, rumbling chuckle. "Gee, Bennet. I never thought of you as a woman who went back on her word." His lips quirked in a teasing smile.

Of course he'd remember the silly promise she'd made the afternoon they'd collected mistletoe. And if they were alone, she just might break it a second time.

Kat wasn't sure if she walked or floated back to the sitting room, but her heart had never been so full.

She sat next to Jack on the aptly named love seat while Elaine topped off everyone's mulled wine.

"Since this is Kat's first time joining us for our Christmas Wish tradition, we'll let her go first," Elaine began, beaming in her direction. "All you have to do is share one wish you'd like to come true before the end of the year."

"Out loud?" Kat asked hesitantly. Weren't you supposed to keep wishes a secret or else they wouldn't come true?

"We don't believe in silly superstitions," Rich added with an air of authority. "Saying a wish out loud gives it power, like an affirmation."

"Okay…" Still uncertain, Kat glanced at Jack.

He gave her a smile of encouragement.

"Let's see…" She toyed with the stem of her glass. One of her wishes had already come true—about five minutes earlier, to be precise. So, she said the only other thing that came to mind. "I wish I could find a way to save Hope Hideaway from closing."

"Hope Hideaway?" Elaine asked.

"It's a women's shelter where I work." She chose not to add that it was also where she lived, not wanting to arouse too many questions.

"It's on the verge of closing?" Rich repeated for clarification.

Jack shifted by her side but remained silent.

"It is, unfortunately. We lost two of our top donors several months ago." Everyone stared at her with open concern bordering on pity, and Kat sank further into the cushions, wishing she'd never mentioned it. "I'm sure something will work out, though."

Jack squirmed as though a feather from one of the down

throw pillows was sticking in his side.

"How are you sure?" Rich prodded. "Do you have a plan of action in place?"

"Um…" Kat glanced at Jack again.

He stared into his glass, his jaw firmly clenched.

"Let's move on," he muttered. "Who's next?"

"Hold on a minute." Rich stood and set down his drink. "How much do you need?"

"I—I beg your pardon?" Kat stammered, heat creeping up her neck.

"Money. How much money does the shelter need to stay open?"

To her surprise, he pulled a leather-bound checkbook from inside his suit jacket.

"Oh, you don't have to—"

"Nonsense." He slipped a Montblanc pen from the same pocket and flipped the checkbook open. "It isn't every Christmas we can make someone's wish come true. This time, we have the means to help and that's exactly what I intend to do. Now, how much do you need?"

Kat heard Jack grind his teeth by her side, but she felt trapped. "I don't know," she murmured helplessly.

"Never mind, then. This should be enough." Rich scribbled a number on the check before tearing it off and handing it to her.

Her cheeks colored at the substantial number of zeros. "Thank you." Her words sounded more like a question than a statement, but Rich didn't seem to notice as he slipped his checkbook and pen back into his pocket.

"Who's next? Tonight, I'm in the business of granting wishes."

Everyone chuckled. Except for Jack.

When she braved another glance, his features were set in hard, grim lines.

And although he sat right next to her, he'd never felt so far away.

CHAPTER 25

*H*is heart pounding, Jack bounded down the front steps two at a time before quickly crossing the driveway in long, determined strides.

Although the bitter night air burned the back of his throat, he filled his lungs, his chest rising and falling faster with each agitated breath.

Sitting through the remainder of his family's Christmas tradition had been agony. Ever since his father whipped out his checkbook, Jack hadn't been able to think straight. Even replaying the incident in his mind caused his muscles to tense.

He tried to muster a smile as he held the passenger door open for Kat, but his lips remained firmly pressed in a thin crease.

For several miles, they drove in deafening silence.

Jack kept his gaze on the dark, misty road ahead.

After a while, icy raindrops pinged against the windshield until they increased in intensity, compelling Jack to flip on the wipers.

The *swish, swish* of the rubber against glass seemed to be telling him something. If he didn't push his anger aside, he wouldn't be able to see clearly.

Of course, that was easier said than done.

His father's financial interference resurfaced old wounds.

And the fact that Kat had accepted the money…

Jack's fingers clenched around the steering wheel.

He couldn't blame her. She wanted to save the shelter. How could he begrudge her that? She didn't know he already had a plan in motion. She also couldn't know his father's check came with strings attached.

And yet, the reality of these facts didn't alleviate the sharp pain in his chest. Or stifle the tiny voice that whispered, *She chose the money over you, just like Ashley.*

He stole a sideways glance in her direction.

Kat stared out the window, although there wasn't much to see. Beyond the water droplets clinging to the glass, darkness stretched into the distance. Her hands rested in her lap, twisting the ends of her scarf into a tight knot.

Jack instantly softened. She wasn't Ashley. And she didn't know the whole story.

"I didn't realize until my senior year of high school that my dad had my entire life planned out for me."

At his hushed confession, she stirred, turning to gaze at him in the dimly lit cab.

"His real estate business had been thriving for a few years by then. And the day before graduation, he brought me into his office and offered me a job with the company." Jack tried to block out visions of that afternoon, but he could still see every detail— the proud expression on his father's face that instantly turned to anger had been seared into his brain.

"The thing is, he already knew I wanted to work at the diner, and possibly own my own place one day. I started as a busboy at Marty's Diner when I was sixteen and worked my way up to a prep cook, then an apprentice."

Jack had spent a few hours every day after school learning everything he could from the retired navy cook. Eventually when he graduated, and his family moved to Primrose Valley, Jack worked full-time as Marty's right-hand man. Marty and his wife, Bernadette, even let Jack stay in the spare room in their home, eventually arranging for Jack to buy the diner—and pay them back in installments—when they moved to Tennessee.

"When I reminded my dad that I wanted to work for Marty, he laughed in my face." Jack cringed at the memory. "He said Ashley would never marry a lowly cook at a diner. And I needed to think seriously about my future."

"That's awful," Kat murmured, her tone pained.

He swallowed, his throat raw, as repressed emotions rose to the surface. "Of course, I told my dad he didn't know what he was talking about. And Ashley and I would be very happy together. That's when he said I'd regret my decision." Jack shook his head. "I thought that was just something people said. I didn't realize it was actually a threat."

"What happened?" she asked tentatively, almost as if she feared the answer.

"The day of graduation—also the day I planned to propose—Ashley told me that my dad offered her a job. Incidentally, the same job he'd offered me. It included a generous salary and a stipend for college. According to Ashley, she'd be foolish to refuse. The catch? The job was in New York, at an East Coast office he'd opened and wanted to expand."

"Oh, Jack," Kat whispered.

"The thing is, my dad told Ashley he'd only given her the job to get under my skin. He was hoping the prospect of losing her would change my mind. But that didn't matter. She said regardless of how the opportunity fell in her lap, it was too good to pass up."

To his surprise, he didn't feel the typical stab of betrayal when he thought about Ashley's decision. That particular wound seemed to have waned over time. But his anger toward his father? That was alive and well.

"I'm telling you this because my dad sees money as a tool to get what he wants. He's not altruistic. There's always an ulterior motive."

She didn't respond as they turned down a tree-lined road, approaching the Morning Glory Inn.

"It's your money," Jack added. "I won't tell you what to do with it. But I thought you should know." He eased into a parking spot and let the engine idle.

They sat in silence a moment, listening to the *swish, swish* of the windshield wipers and raindrops pitter-patter against the roof of the truck.

While he felt a sense of relief in sharing his past with Kat, it also stirred unpleasant emotions he wasn't sure how to process. And while his anger and frustration wasn't directed at her, he struggled to untangle tonight's situation from everything else with his father. He needed time to sort it out.

Lifting the collar of his coat, he reached for the handle, bracing himself for the downpour. "Come on. I'll walk you to the door."

*N*ot until Jack's taillights disappeared in the darkness did Kat allow the first tear to fall.

For several minutes, she didn't bother going inside. Shivering on the front porch, she watched the rain pummel the wet earth as tears stained her cheeks.

There was so much she wanted to say to Jack. So, why couldn't she find the words? They lodged in the back of her throat, leaving her to flail helplessly.

Meanwhile, the check scorched a hole in her pocket.

She didn't want Rich Gardener's money, especially after everything Jack told her. But how could she turn it down, knowing what it would mean to Fern and the shelter?

Retrieving the offending slip of paper, she held it in her hands. The trail of zeros glared up at her accusingly.

She didn't doubt Jack's claims that his father's money would come with strings attached. She'd seen it before. In the past, potential donors had offered Fern generous sums, but wanted to tell her how to run the shelter and control her decisions. They'd also suggested she support specific political candidates, even going so far as encouraging her to influence the voting habits of Hope Hideaway residents.

Without hesitation, Fern had shown them the door. And even on the verge of losing everything, Kat knew she would make the same choice.

Closing her eyes, she pinched both ends of the check and swiftly ripped it in half, praying for some of Fern's hopeful optimism.

Because in that moment, the world had never looked so bleak.

CHAPTER 26

*K*at groaned as she pawed the nightstand, attempting to silence her ringing cell phone.

"Hello?" she croaked without checking caller ID.

"We solved it!" Penny shrieked. "Hurry! I have a feeling this is the one. But I don't want to check without you."

Despite her low spirits, a glimmer of excitement rippled through her. After dressing quickly, Kat raced out the front door.

As she skipped around shimmering puddles on the way to her car, her heaviness began to lift. Warm sunlight filtered through the damp tree branches, and as she tilted her chin toward the periwinkle sky, she inhaled the fresh, invigorating fragrance of an early morning after the rain—the scent of hope and second chances.

By the time she'd reached Penny's place, she'd resolved to go to Jack's directly afterward to tell him she'd destroyed the check. She could still see the pained look in his eyes from last night, and she would do anything to restore his usual warmth and playful glimmer.

"Come in, come in." Penny ushered her inside, beaming like the embodiment of pure joy. "I agonized over the clue all night, then I went to The Calendar Café for a cinnamon roll, and before long, nearly everyone in town was trying to help me solve it."

Walking briskly, Penny led the way into her father's old room. "Frank figured out the first line, 'the seven seas I used to sail,' referenced a boat, most likely a sailing ship. And Maggie, who's taken up bird-watching in her retirement, surmised that the second line, 'the sky was once my stage,' referred to a bird of some kind. Or more specifically, a *feather* since the line is in the past tense.

"Of course, it was Beverly who pieced together the rest," she added. "'But the greatest story I'll regale, belongs upon the page.'"

"A book?" Kat asked.

"Close." Standing at her father's desk, Penny lifted a small rectangular wooden box with the silhouette of a sailing ship hand painted on the lid. "None of the clues made sense until I remembered this." She unhinged a tiny gold latch and flipped it open.

A feather-plumed ink pen nestled on a bed of burgundy velvet.

As all the pieces came together, Kat's pulse quickened. "Do you see the brooch?"

Please, please be there. She didn't think she could handle another clue. With Christmas only a few weeks away, they were running out of time.

"No..." Penny ran her finger along the perimeter of the box. "But..."

"But what?" Kat pressed, inching closer.

She spotted a tip of burgundy ribbon wedged between the inner velvet lining and the wooden exterior.

Pinching the frayed edge, Penny tugged. The entire base resting beneath the pen shifted, separating from the box to reveal a hidden compartment underneath.

Penny and Kat gasped in unison as they glimpsed a sprig of mistletoe crafted from gleaming gold and gemstones.

"I can't believe it," Kat murmured. "It's even more beautiful than I imagined."

"Here." Penny passed her the box. "You've waited long enough."

Taking it gingerly, Kat blinked back tears. "Thank you," she whispered, suddenly too overcome with emotion to speak.

"Do you want to call Fern with the good news?"

"Yes! Of course." Sniffling, she dug into her coat pocket for her cell phone, unable to tear her gaze from the sparkling stones.

Fern picked up on the first ring. But before she could say anything, Kat blurted, "We found it, Fern! We actually found it!"

"Found what?"

"Helena's brooch. The answer to our problem. A miracle!"

"Slow down, mija. You're not making any sense."

Grinning broadly, Kat paced the room, too excited to stand still. "I didn't tell you before because I didn't want to get your hopes up. But I came to Poppy Creek hoping to find the brooch Helena always talked about." Kat glanced at her open palm, still stunned by the brooch's beauty. "It took Penny and me a while to find it, but it was worth the wait. It's gorgeous. And I know it'll sell for enough money to keep the shelter open, at least until we can find more donors."

She paused, waiting for Fern's reaction.

But instead of a jubilant exclamation, she murmured, "Oh, mija...."

"What's wrong?" Kat stopped pacing, and Penny shot her a curious glance.

"I'm so sorry." Fern's voice fell away and Kat strained her ear against the speaker.

"I don't understand. Why are you sorry?"

"It's very sweet what you two girls did. But... the brooch isn't worth very much."

"What do you mean? It has to be! All these diamonds and gems—"

"They're not real."

The room started to spin, and Kat sank onto the twin bed, the springs creaking beneath her weight. "What?"

"They're imitations."

"They can't be," Kat argued, her chest tightening. "The way Helena went on and on about it, I thought—" She scrunched her eyes shut, her temples beginning to throb. "How do you know it's not real?"

"Because your mother told me. The same night she admitted that mourning the loss of the brooch was simply a transference, a less painful way to grieve her greatest loss—the love she left behind."

At Fern's words, a small sob escaped Kat's lips.

Penny rushed to her side, placing a comforting hand on her shoulder, although she could hear only one half of the conversation.

"It was a gift from Penny's father on their wedding day," Fern explained. "It wasn't the monetary value that made the brooch special. It was the meaning behind it."

Kat sat motionless, too distraught to speak. She couldn't even answer when Fern called her name, worry etched into her voice.

Finally, Kat managed to whisper, "I'm sorry, I have to go."

And with that, she hung up the phone.

Leaning against her sister, she cried until she had no more tears left.

❄

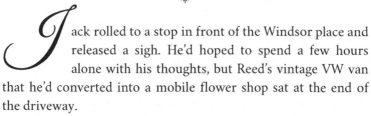

ack rolled to a stop in front of the Windsor place and released a sigh. He'd hoped to spend a few hours alone with his thoughts, but Reed's vintage VW van that he'd converted into a mobile flower shop sat at the end of the driveway.

Jack opened the passenger door of the truck, and Fitz hopped to the ground. He sniffed the air a moment before bounding behind the house, his tail wagging.

As Jack rounded the corner, he laughed when he spotted Reed squatting down to pet Fitz, only to receive a slobbery greeting.

"It's nice to see you, too, buddy." Reed scratched the scruff around Fitz's neck before standing and wiping the slime from his face with his sleeve.

Fitz proceeded to roll around in a shallow puddle, caking his white coat in mud.

Jack groaned. That would take some time to scrub out.

"Hey, Fitz enjoys the dirt as much as I do," Reed said with a grin.

"Don't encourage him."

"What are you two doing out here?" Reed asked, retrieving his sketchbook from the ground by his feet.

"I thought I'd pull up a few broken planks from the front porch before heading in to work. What about you?"

"Sketching out some landscaping ideas. I can tell there used to be an impressive garden back here at one time. And check out the gazebo." He nodded toward a structure covered in wilted vines. "It's still in pretty decent shape."

"Great," Jack muttered. "At least one thing in my life isn't falling apart."

"Meeting the family didn't go well?" Reed led the way to the expansive back porch where he'd left a tall Coleman thermos.

"Actually, it went great. Until my dad offered Kat money." Jack flopped onto the top step, watching Fitz dig a sizable hole in the middle of the backyard.

"What? Why would he do that?" Reed poured hot chocolate into a plastic cup and handed it to Jack.

"To tick me off, no doubt."

"I'm sorry, man." Using the thermos lid as his own cup, Reed settled a few steps down. "How does Kat feel about it?"

"To be honest, I was so caught up in my own stuff, I haven't asked her."

Reed nodded, contemplating Jack's admission as he took a sip.

"It's strange," Jack continued thoughtfully. "It's like my anger toward my dad blinds me from everything else. I don't know why I let him affect me like that."

"I get it. When I found out about my dad's affair, I didn't speak to him for almost two years. We've only barely started to patch things up."

"What made you want to try?"

Reed stared into his hot chocolate a moment before answering. "For a while, I thought my anger was some form of justice for what he'd done. But it turns out, I wasn't just punishing my dad. My whole family suffered."

Jack thought about all the times Lucy had begged him to work things out with their dad. And last night, he'd been reminded of how much he missed everyone—how much he needed them in his life.

"What's it like between you and your father now?" Remembering the hot chocolate in his hand, Jack took a sip. While delicious, it lacked a certain hint of spice he'd become accustomed to.

"Not great, but it's better than it was. It'll take time to rebuild what was broken. But we're working on it."

"I'm glad. You're a better man than I am."

Reed flashed a teasing grin. "I've been saying that for years."

"Ha!" Jack snorted. "Just for that, I'm not going to tell you that Fitz is digging a crater-sized hole in the backyard."

Startled, Reed followed Jack's gaze, shaking his head in bemusement. "I guess I know where I'm planting the cherry tree."

They shared a chuckle before Reed offered, "You can leave Fitz here with me while you're gone."

"Gone where?"

"Well, the way I see it, there are two conversations you need to have. One with Kat. And one with your dad."

CHAPTER 27

*K*at crumpled the damp tissue in her lap as Penny handed her a steaming cup of chamomile tea before sitting on the bed beside her.

"I'm so sorry," Kat murmured. "I feel terrible for wasting your time."

"Don't be silly. I loved spending time with you. And the treasure hunt made my dad feel close by again. Truthfully, I think he'd be glad we got to solve it together."

Although her eyes were red and raw, Kat sensed the onset of more tears. She quickly sipped her tea, allowing the warm honey-sweetened liquid to soothe her swollen throat.

"But there is something I don't understand," Penny added, her brow furrowed. "Why didn't Helena tell you the brooch wasn't worth anything when you asked her if you could sell it?"

Nausea swept over Kat, and with trembling hands, she set the china teacup on the nightstand. She'd known this moment would arise eventually. But the inevitability didn't make it any less terrifying.

"I... haven't been completely honest with you," Kat confessed, her tone faint and tentative.

"What do you mean?"

"Helena didn't tell me because I technically didn't ask for her permission."

Penny raised her eyebrows in confusion, and Kat took a deep breath, trying to steady her frantic heartbeat.

She'd thought waiting to tell Penny would make it easier, but it had only made it a thousand times harder. She'd come to care deeply for the woman beside her. Not only did she hate the thought of causing her pain, she feared losing her trust.

Or worse... losing her altogether.

"I'm so sorry I've kept this from you. There's no excuse. I—" Kat faltered as her throat constricted around the words. Forcing herself to continue, she swallowed. "Helena passed away several years ago. And I'm so unbelievably sorry I didn't tell you sooner."

For close to an eternity, Penny didn't speak. She didn't move. Or even seem to be breathing. Finally, she whispered, "How?"

"How?" Kat repeated, not sure what she meant.

"How did she die?" Penny's voice sounded far away, and her eyes glazed over, full of pain.

Unable to bear it, Kat dropped her gaze to her lap, picking at the frayed fringe of her scarf. "It was... an overdose."

Penny sucked in a sharp breath before asking, "Why didn't you tell me?"

"I—I couldn't. Not without..." Her cheeks flamed as all her guilt and shame flooded to the surface.

"Not without what?" Penny's tone softened, exuding compassion.

Her kindness made Kat's confession all the more difficult. Once she revealed the terrible truth she'd been hiding, her sister would never see her the same way again.

"I'm the one who found her," she finally admitted in a ghostly whisper.

"Oh, Kat." Penny placed a hand on her forearm, her eyes glistening.

"I thought she was sleeping at first. I called her name a few times, and when I finally realized she wasn't going to wake up, I —" Her voice broke, and she buried her face in her hands, unable to go on.

Penny wrapped an arm around her protectively.

"I yelled at her," Kat confessed with a sob, her heart wrenching at the ugly admission. "I hated her for leaving me. I was so angry." Tears slid down her cheeks, but she didn't bother wiping them away. "How could I admit something so awful? I honestly wouldn't blame you if you never wanted to speak to me again."

To her surprise, her sister wrapped her arms around her even tighter, holding her for several still moments as their tears fell in tandem. "I'm so sorry, Kat. No child should have to go through something like that. And for what it's worth, I was angry at her, too."

"Was?" Kat sniffled.

"I held on to my anger for a long time. But honestly, it was exhausting. And it wouldn't bring her back. She'd left us without a second thought. Or at least, that's what I'd always thought." Kat's gaze drifted to the brooch, now resting beside her lukewarm tea on the nightstand. In a strange way, it had given them both a piece of a different kind of puzzle—their mother. Maybe Helena wasn't as cold and callous as they'd always assumed.

"Will you tell me about her?" Penny asked softly, her tone tentative but hopeful.

Kat had resisted for so long, but unexpectedly, a smile rose from somewhere deep within her.

"We're going to need some more tea."

*T*hey went through two pots of tea, laughing and crying on the chaise lounge in the living room as Kat shared her memories. And as she told each story, Helena began to take shape in her mind as a more rounded, nuanced person. Perhaps things weren't as black-and-white as she'd once believed.

Although the experience was cathartic for both women, Kat needed more. Her picture of Helena still seemed incomplete.

She set her teacup on the coffee table, and turned to Penny. "I have to go."

"Go?"

"Back to Starcross Cove."

Penny slowly set her cup beside Kat's. "For how long?"

"Long enough to find some answers." She didn't elaborate, knowing her sister would understand. Some pieces of the puzzle remained missing.

"What about Jack?"

The mere mention of his name sent a pang of remorse rippling through her. It had only been a few hours, but she already missed him. "Can you give him something for me? It will explain why I have to go."

"But you'll be back?" Penny's voice strained with a mixture of hope and hesitation.

"Of course. My only sister has a wedding on the horizon."

"We'll set the date for tomorrow, if it'll bring you back."

Kat laughed softly, despite the ache in her heart.

Saying goodbye to Penny and walking out of Thistle & Thorn felt like leaving a part of herself behind. And a fresh tear escaped with each footstep that led her farther away.

She might be heading back to Starcross Cove…

But she was no longer heading home.

*a*s Jack strode briskly down Main Street toward Thistle & Thorn, his legs itched to break into a full-on run. He couldn't wait to see her, to hold her ... maybe more. The kiss they'd shared beneath the mistletoe had replayed in his mind since last night. He didn't use the term *life-changing* lightly, but that's exactly how he would describe it.

His steps slowed as he neared the entrance and a familiar fabric arrested his attention. A houndstooth scarf dangled from the doorjamb. It must have gotten caught when Kat went inside.

He smiled to himself, recalling the afternoon they'd met.

When he turned the knob, rescuing her scarf once again, he noticed a long tear. His heart sank. He'd have to find a way to fix it.

"Jack." Penny called his name as he entered, but her voice lacked its usual warmth.

"Hey, Heart." He glanced around the shop, scanning the festive decorations and unique knickknacks and collectibles.

Before he could ask, Penny told him, "She isn't here. She... went back to Starcross Cove."

In his shock, he nearly stumbled over a wicker basket filled with umbrellas.

"But she left you this," she added with a kind, sympathetic smile. "She said you'd know what it meant."

Penny handed him a dusty CD case. When he peered closer at the blue-tinted photograph of a woman on the cover, he noticed the words in the upper left-hand corner.

BLUE

JONI MITCHELL

His pulse quickening, he turned the case over, skimming the list of song titles until his gaze rested on the eighth one.

River.

A slow smile spread across his face.

"What does it mean?" Penny asked, peering at him curiously. "There's something I need to do."

CHAPTER 28

*T*he dulcet, melancholy notes of Joni Mitchell's "River" filled the cab of Jack's truck as he rumbled along the familiar road with his windows cracked open. He relished the icy chill whipping past him, promising another snowstorm on the horizon.

Poppy Creek usually saw only a couple of snowstorms a year, and Jack looked forward to every single one. Something about witnessing the entire world enveloped in white reminded him of a blank slate.

And now more than ever, he appreciated the comparison.

Even though he drove alone, he sensed Kat's presence. He could almost hear her captivating voice harmonizing with each line of the song, encouraging him to take this leap of faith and forgiveness.

She may not fully realize it, but she was the embodiment of Fern's sage wisdom. Kat had the most generous heart he'd ever known. And he longed for the moment he could tell her exactly that.

But before he could look to the future, he needed to face his past.

When he rang the doorbell, and the melodic chime echoed inside, Jack expected the housekeeper to greet him. He wasn't prepared for his father's startled expression.

"Jack?" Once the shock settled, Rich stepped to the side, allowing his son to enter. "Were we expecting you?"

"Nope. I was just passing by." Jack cringed as he moved into the expansive foyer. *Just passing by? Really?* Man, he was terrible at this.

Michael Bublé's "I'll Be Home for Christmas" drifted down the hallway along with the sweet scent of sugar cookies.

"Your mom and Lucy are baking in the kitchen," Rich explained, noticing the not-so-subtle way Jack sniffed the air.

Incredulous, Jack inhaled deeply, detecting the faintest whiff of almond extract—his mother's secret ingredient. He'd assumed she didn't bake anymore. Wasn't that why she'd hired the private chef with a flair for French pastries?

He tried to refocus on Kat's words from the other night, remembering why he was there.

Love is generous. It chooses to see the good in people.

There were times it felt like he'd need a magnifying glass to find the good in his father. But he also knew years of holding a grudge could cloud a person's perspective.

"I'm starting my New Year's resolution a few weeks early," he said, mustering up his nerve. "It's a new trend called *talking about your feelings.*"

Rich's eyes widened.

"I still haven't worked out all the kinks, but I'll give it my best shot." Jack drew in a fortifying breath, squaring his shoulders. "Ever since your business took off, it seemed like the success changed you—changed *us*, as a family. But the real kicker was when you offered Ashley the job in New York. That crushed me, Dad." His throat tightened, but he forced himself to push through the discomfort. "It may seem foolish to ask after all these years, but I have to know… why'd you do it? The real, honest answer. Why'd you offer her the job?"

For several minutes, Rich didn't respond. And when he finally met Jack's gaze, his eyes were filled with sorrow. "Because I knew she'd take it."

Silence stretched between them.

"I don't understand."

Rich sighed, deep and pained. "I offered her the job because I knew she'd never stay in Poppy Creek. Not long term, anyway. And if you'd married her like you'd planned, it would've hurt a whole lot more when she walked away."

Jack winced, wounded by his father's words as though they'd been an actual blow to the gut. "Why didn't you just tell me?"

"Would you have listened to me if I had?"

As Jack pondered his father's question, uneasiness settled in the pit of his stomach because he honestly wasn't sure.

"Look, son. I have my share of regrets," Rich admitted with some effort. "I may have stepped in when I shouldn't have. And it would be a lie to tell you that my pride and disappointment didn't play into my decision."

Jack's spirits fell at his father's admission, and it took every ounce of strength to stay positive. *Look for the good....*

"You may not believe this," Rich continued, his voice hoarse, "but you're still my son, and I love you. My greatest regret is losing you and letting my arrogance prevent me from fixing my mistakes. Having you here last night made me realize how wrong I've been. And how much time I've thrown away."

Jack stared, dumbfounded. He'd never heard his dad apologize. Or speak so freely about his feelings.

"Tell me what I can do to make it right."

Jack hesitated. He'd waited most of his life to hear his father say those words. And during the countless times he'd played out the conversation in his mind, he'd had plenty to say in return.

But now, standing before the man who'd caused him so much

pain, Jack had no desire to lash out. Or make his father grovel. "I'm sorry I've been so stubborn. We should've had this conversation years ago."

"What changed?" Rich asked. "Or let me guess… a certain beguiling redhead with pipes like Judy Garland?"

Jack grinned. "Something like that."

"This time," Rich said with an air of humility. "I'll simply *tell* you my advice. Don't let this one get away."

"I don't plan on it."

*T*he entire drive back to Hope Hideaway, Kat thought of Jack. She wanted to call and ask if he'd spoken with his father and if he wanted to talk about it. But she wasn't sure what to say when he inevitably asked about her return.

She didn't have a plan.

Kat knew two things: She needed to look through Helena's hope chest—a task she'd been avoiding since her mother passed away. And she needed to help Fern find a way to save the shelter.

Penny, bless her heart, had offered the tiny nest egg she and Colt had been saving to buy a house. But Kat couldn't accept. She had to believe God would provide another way—a miracle, as Fern put it.

As thoughts of Fern flooded her mind, Kat's grip on the steering wheel relaxed. She looked forward to seeing the woman who always knew exactly what to say. Although, Kat suspected her soothing words may have more to do with the love behind them than the words themselves.

Fern's greeting when she arrived—an enveloping hug and heaping plate of Milagros—instantly calmed her troubled heart.

Kat may not be home anymore, but she was definitely with family.

"How was the drive, mija? Are you hungry? I have tamales. Or I can heat up a bowl of posole?"

"The cookies are perfect, thank you." As Kat shrugged out of her coat, her hand flew to her throat. "My scarf! I must have dropped it somewhere."

Her mind flashed to the first afternoon she'd met Jack, and her chest suddenly ached.

"Oh, that reminds me." Fern scurried to the table in the entryway and returned with a brown shopping bag with a telltale red ribbon on the handle.

Clara Holland had opened The Red Ribbon Gift Shoppe in honor of her late grandmother, who always wrapped her presents with a shiny red ribbon. The store quickly became Starcross Cove's go-to spot for special, one-of-a-kind gifts.

As Kat settled on the couch, Fern handed her the bag, a delighted smile on her lips.

"But you already sent me my Christmas present," Kat reminded her. "The perfume."

"This isn't from me." Fern settled on the armchair by the fireplace, her eyes twinkling.

"Then who is it from?"

"I don't know. Clara said she got a call from a gentleman this afternoon looking for a very specific item. When she told him she had it, he paid for it over the phone and asked if he could pay extra to have it delivered."

Her heart racing, Kat reached for the bow. "He didn't leave a message?"

"He gave Clara his name with his credit card, but said you wouldn't need it."

"How strange...." Her heart soared with hope as she tugged the end of the ribbon and it slipped to the floor.

The second she glimpsed the gift nestled in red tissue paper, tears sprang to her eyes.

"What is it?" Fern asked, leaning forward.

Kat lifted the beautiful, feather-soft scarf from the bag and brought it to her cheek, nuzzling the silky fabric.

The plaid pattern—so synonymous with the gift's sender—couldn't have been more perfect.

"You're glowing." Fern smiled as Kat wrapped the scarf around her neck. "It must be from someone pretty special."

"It is. And I can't wait to tell you all about him."

CHAPTER 29

*a*s Kat kneeled before the dusty leather trunk, she toyed with the fringe of her scarf.

She knew she'd come back to Hope Hideaway for this very reason, but she still couldn't bring herself to open it.

The creaking of the attic steps drew her attention to the narrow doorway. Fern emerged carrying two mugs of hot chocolate. "I thought it would be chilly up here."

Kat smiled, recognizing the excuse to lend moral support. She gratefully accepted the offering, taking a languid sip as Fern eased herself onto a worn armchair in need of new upholstery.

After setting the mug on the scuffed hardwood, Kat flipped open the brass latch. She held her breath as she slowly eased open the lid, scattering specks of dust.

When her gaze fell on the first item resting on top, a small gasp escaped. "Is that…?" Her question trailed off as she caressed the smooth cotton, her fingertips traveling to the name embroidered along the edge in pink thread.

Katherine.

"Your mother made that in an embroidery class at the community center," Fern told her with a wistful smile. "I remember hearing her mutter under her breath each time she stuck herself with the needle. But she was determined to finish it for you."

Misty-eyed, Kat grazed the uneven stitching. "I never actually liked my name," she admitted, recalling how she'd asked to go by Kat at a young age.

"Do you know what it means?"

Kat shook her head, still studying each line of thread painstakingly put in place by her mother's hand.

"It means *pure*."

"Pure?" Kat echoed, not feeling a connection to that description at all. "What an odd thing to name a baby. But then, knowing Helena, she probably named me after some celebrity."

Fern sipped her hot chocolate before responding, her voice soft and steady. "Your mother scoured baby naming websites nearly every night for a month. When I asked her why she was having so much trouble deciding, you know what she said?"

Sensing that the question was rhetorical, Kat leaned back on her heels, waiting for Fern to continue.

"She said she wanted to do everything in her power to make sure your life didn't turn out like hers." Fern sniffled, drying her eyes with the collar of her sweater. "She remained clean and sober for the entire pregnancy. And I thought—I prayed—it would last. When she relapsed, my faith wavered. I couldn't understand what went wrong. In the end, only the Lord knows a person's heart. But He gave me an incredible gift amid the heartache."

Kat fought back tears, wondering what possible silver lining Fern could have found.

"He gave me you, mija." A solitary tear tumbled down her weathered cheek, and the sob Kat had been holding back broke through her wall of restraint.

Rushing to Fern's side, she threw her arms around the

woman's neck, not caring about the awkward position or the precarious cup of hot chocolate resting in her lap.

For so long, she'd focused on what she didn't have. And yet, this whole time, she'd had Fern, who'd given her a mother's love, no matter what it said on her birth certificate.

Life could be messy and heartbreaking, but it was also wonderful.

When Kat pulled away, Fern set down her mug and rose from the chair. "Come with me. There's something I want to show you."

Kat followed her to the other side of the attic, surprised when Fern paused in front of another hope chest. "Helena had two?"

"This one is yours."

Kat blinked in confusion. Since she was technically a Hope Hideaway employee, not a resident, she never had her own hope chest.

"I started adding things here and there shortly after your mother passed away. I always intended to give it to you when you were ready to leave home."

Kat stared, too overwhelmed to speak.

"Open it." Fern gave her a loving nudge.

Kneeling in front of the steamer trunk, Kat admired the rich, chocolatey leather and shiny brass lock. But as beautiful as she found the exterior, she wasn't prepared for what she discovered inside.

Recipe cards filled with Fern's favorites, including her top secret Pequeños Milagros, a conch shell so she could hear the ocean no matter where she went, and…

"My own molinillo!" Kat cried, plucking it from among the other items.

"In case you want to carry on the tradition."

As Kat reminisced about the first time she'd made Fern's hot chocolate for Jack, a smile sprang to her lips.

"Or maybe you already have…."

Kat blushed. "This would have made it easier." As she ran her palm along the smooth wood, the reality of Fern's gesture settled over her.

Fern was giving her permission to leave Hope Hideaway.

A lump rose in her throat, and she couldn't bring herself to say the words out loud.

Sensing her troubled thoughts, Fern knelt beside her. "This isn't goodbye, mija. No matter what happens or where you go, you'll always be my daughter."

"But I can't leave. Not now. Not when the shelter—"

"We'll be okay." Fern gently wiped a tear from Kat's cheek. "There's still hope. But right now, it's time for you to stop hiding, and go and live your life."

Before Kat could answer, a faint cough startled them both.

Ann—the newest Hope Hideaway resident—lingered in the doorway. "I'm sorry, Fern. But there's a man here to see you. He says it's important."

❄

*K*at followed Fern into the living room, her heart thrumming. For a fleeting moment, she wondered if the mysterious visitor was Jack.

But she didn't recognize the stout, middle-aged man standing in front of the fireplace, briefcase in hand. He turned when they entered, giving them both a friendly smile. "This is a lovely place you have here."

"Thank you," Fern responded with her usual warm, welcoming demeanor. "How can I help you…?" Her voice carried a questioning lilt.

"Paul. Paul Volt. I hope you don't mind the intrusion, but I have an important matter to discuss with you." He flipped open his briefcase. "I'm here on behalf of an anonymous donor who's set up a trust fund for Hope Hideaway. A fixed amount will be transferred to your account every month for as long as the shelter remains open. I've done extensive research to ensure the amount surpasses your monthly operational costs, and I hope you find it more than satisfactory."

Kat's gaze flew to Fern, who looked as shocked as she felt.

"If there's a place where we can sign papers," Paul continued, "I can begin the first transfer of funds."

As if floating on a cloud, Fern led them into the kitchen.

While Paul laid out the paperwork on the expansive island, Fern arranged cookies on a plate, still in a daze.

Concerned Rich Gardener might be trying to circumvent her refusal of his check, Kat asked, "Mr. Volt—"

"Call me Paul," he said cheerily, helping himself to a cookie as Fern started a fresh batch of hot chocolate.

"Paul," she corrected, "is there any fine print that gives the donor input over the way Fern runs the shelter?"

"Absolutely not. My client specifically stipulated that the funds were to be used at Miss Flores's discretion."

Kat breathed a little easier, but her mind raced to surmise who the donor might be. Her thoughts kept drifting to Jack, but where would he get that kind of money?

"Is there a reason the donor wishes to remain anonymous?" she asked. "We'd love to thank them."

Paul hesitated mid-bite. Swallowing, he answered, "No nefarious reason. My client is simply a private man, particularly when it comes to finances and things of this nature."

"That's very admirable," Fern said, speaking for the first time since they entered the kitchen. "Please tell your client that we're extremely grateful." Beaming brightly, she handed him a mug of steaming hot chocolate.

"It will be my pleasure." Paul inhaled the sweet and spicy scent curling from the rim. "This smells incredible."

"It's a family recipe, passed down from generation to generation." Fern turned her smile on Kat, who grinned back, her heart full.

At the beginning of December, she'd left Starcross Cove hoping to find a way to save the shelter.

And now that she had the answer to her prayers, she realized she'd found so much more than she ever imagined.

CHAPTER 30

*S*tanding on Main Street, gazing at the quaint town in all its fanciful, festive garb, Kat knew she'd come home.

Wrapping her new scarf around her neck, she traced the same path she'd walked her first day in Poppy Creek. Only this time, her footsteps were light, not weighed down by fear and uncertainty.

She hugged the hefty tote bag by her side, eager to see Penny's expression when she revealed its contents. Not to mention the look on her sister's face when she announced her good news.

In truth, she'd wanted to tell Jack first. But the items she had for Penny couldn't wait.

And she and Jack had the rest of their lives.

The mere thought gave her goose bumps.

As she pushed through the front door of Thistle & Thorn, and the welcoming bell jingled overhead, a huge smile swept across her face. Oh, how she'd missed this place.

Penny glanced up from helping a customer, and a gleeful squeal escaped her lips. "You're back!" Quickly excusing herself, Penny enveloped Kat in a warm, sisterly embrace.

Kat hugged her tightly, overwhelmed by the sudden flood of

affection. Sniffling, she pulled back, trying to compose herself. "I brought you something."

Penny shot her customer a sheepish glance. "Frida, would you mind if we—"

"Not at all, dear. I'll come back later." The elderly woman shuffled past them, her eyes glinting with her latest piece of gossip. In a few hours, the entire town would know Kat had returned.

Which meant Kat needed to be quick if she wanted to reach Jack before the rumor mill.

Penny flipped the Closed sign and led the way upstairs.

Although she'd been gone only a few days, Kat relished being back in Penny's apartment. She'd become accustomed to its coziness and quirky charm.

"Would you like some tea?" Penny asked, setting another log on the hearth before prodding the embers.

"No, thanks. I can't stay long. I have to—"

"Find Jack?" Penny cut in, her eyes twinkling.

Kat answered with a coy smile as she lugged the tote bag over to the chaise lounge. "First, I want to show you something."

When Penny sat beside her, Kat handed her a small rectangular scrapbook.

"What is it?" Penny asked, peering curiously at the nondescript cream cover.

"Open it." Kat's stomach fluttered, anticipating her sister's reaction.

The second Penny cracked the spine, she gasped.

A snapshot of a smiling couple cradling an infant gazed up at her.

"It can't be...."

"I found it in Helena's hope chest."

"I can't believe it," Penny murmured, misty-eyed as she slowly turned the pages of her baby album.

After a few minutes, Kat reached into the tote bag, retrieving a second binder. "There's more."

Setting the ivory satin album on Penny's lap, she flipped to the first page, revealing a photo of Helena and Timothy Heart sharing a tender kiss on the front steps of a chapel.

"Their wedding album?" Penny's question carried a note of disbelief.

"Did you know they were married on Christmas Day?"

"I didn't. But it looks... perfect." Her voice broke as she stared at the white steepled church veiled in snow. A simple wreath with a red satin bow hung on the front door and crimson poinsettias lined the stone steps. "Her dress is stunning. I've never seen anything quite like it. If I had to guess, I'd say it's from the 1920s."

For a moment, both women silently admired *The Great Gatsby*–inspired beaded bodice and slimming silhouette.

"Are those..." Leaning forward, Penny squinted at the Polaroid. "Are those feathers along the hemline?"

"See for yourself." Barely able to contain her excitement, Kat stood and pulled the last item from the canvas bag.

As the silvery fabric unfurled, sunlight shimmered off the intricate beadwork, causing it to glitter like diamonds.

Penny sucked in a breath as the feathery hem floated to the floor.

"What do you think?" Kat asked, smiling wide. "I'm pretty sure you two were the same size."

"You mean..." Penny met her gaze, her eyes glistening.

"I think she would've wanted you to have it."

As a solitary tear slid down her cheek, Penny gently brushed the feathers with her fingertips. "Remember how I told you my father described Helena as some magical creature out of a fairy tale?"

Kat nodded.

"He said she had a haunting, angelic voice and enormous,

billowing wings that could carry them through the stars." Another tear followed the first, but she didn't wipe them away. "I never told anyone this, but I'd always imagined her wings were silver, as though they'd been dipped in stardust." Lost in her thoughts, she caressed the soft plumes.

"Do you want to try it on?" Kat asked gently, touched by her sister's story.

"More than anything," she murmured, then her expression brightened. "But first, I just had an impulsive, irrational, and completely wonderful idea." She bolted from the chaise lounge, suddenly bursting with energy.

"What is it?" Kat asked cautiously, wary of her sister's abrupt change in demeanor. Not to mention the wild glint in her eyes.

Even Chip looked concerned as he poked his head out of his enclosure to watch Penny pace the carpet.

"It would require some last-minute planning, which isn't ideal. But it doesn't have to be anything elaborate. Of course, we did just have Frank and Beverly's wedding, but I'm sure they wouldn't mind if—"

"Whoa! Hold on," Kat interrupted. "I'm not following you."

"I want to get married on Christmas Day!" Penny cried, clasping her hands in excitement. "At the chapel. Just like my parents."

Stunned, it took Kat a minute to respond. "You realize that doesn't give you much time to prepare."

"Yes, but we wouldn't need a lot! We could have a simple ceremony in the afternoon. And in lieu of a reception, we can all go to the Christmas Carnival in the evening. Actually, now that I think about it, it's rather perfect. And I know Colt will love the idea."

As Kat mulled it over, Penny added, "We don't need a big bridal party, either. Just a best man and a maid of honor to stand up with us."

"That would certainly make things easier."

"Of course, that's assuming you can come back on Christmas Day. To be my maid of honor," Penny added with a hopeful smile.

For a moment, Kat couldn't speak. Only a few weeks earlier, this woman had been a stranger. And now, Kat not only had a sister, she'd gained a best friend. "I wouldn't miss it for the world," she said at last, her voice thick with emotion. "And I'll definitely be here because... I've decided to stay in Poppy Creek."

Grinning through her tears, Penny shouted, "Did you hear that, Chip? She's staying! Didn't I tell you she would?"

For the second time that afternoon, Kat found herself in an embrace. "I guess it's too late to mention that I'm not really a hugger," she teased, realizing how much she'd come to appreciate the show of affection.

"Oh, it's absolutely too late," Penny laughed. "And you'd better get used to it because it'll be happening a lot. I'm so excited you're staying!"

"There's just one tiny problem...." Kat paused, trying to decide how to phrase her question.

"What's wrong?"

"Nothing's wrong, per se. But I'd need a job. I was wondering if you could use some help around here until I can find something a little more permanent?"

"Are you kidding? I would love that! I haven't been able to find anyone since Bri left for college. And working together would be so much fun!" Penny's grin widened as another idea struck her. "Plus, you could live here!"

"That's a sweet offer, but I thought Colt was moving in after the wedding so you could save up for a house?"

"He was, but then Beverly offered us her place for next to nothing. It's a darling little cottage by the creek. And Chip will have his own room, which he's thrilled about. So, you can stay here, work for me part-time, and—" She snapped her mouth shut as though she were on the verge of saying something she shouldn't.

"And...?" Kat pressed, suddenly curious.

"I'm not supposed to say anything. Jack wants to be the one to tell you."

"Tell me what?"

※

*A*fter cutting down all the dead vines wrapped around the eaves of the Windsor house, Jack stood back to survey his handiwork. Warmth spread across his chest.

It would take several months before the place would be up and running, but he enjoyed watching the progress. What started as an endeavor to help Kat achieve her dream had transformed into so much more.

Her generous nature had inspired him to share what he had with others. And an inn would certainly be a blessing to Poppy Creek. Not only would it alleviate some of the pressure off of George and Trudy, but it would bring more traffic to local businesses.

Jack chuckled, realizing that for once, his goals were aligned with Mayor Burns's—perhaps the real Christmas miracle.

Opening an inn would solve another problem, too. He'd decided to ask Colt to run the inn's restaurant, which would give his friend free rein over the menu, and he and Vick could go back to serving unpretentious comfort food at the diner.

Overall, it was a win-win.

"What do you think, Fitz? How does it look?"

From his lounging position on the front porch, Fitz glanced up from his well-gnawed antler and barked his approval.

Tires crunched across the gravel, drawing the pup's attention toward the driveway. His ears perked up, and in one leap, he bounded down the steps.

Jack turned, his heart ricocheting into his throat as Kat's

Corolla came to a stop beside his truck. He knew he'd missed her, but seeing her again multiplied his emotions tenfold.

Without thinking, he strode toward her, nearly breaking into a jog.

The instant she stepped from the car, he scooped her into his arms, capturing her mouth with his.

She melted against him, only breaking away after Fitz pawed her leg.

"Gee," she gasped, struggling to catch her breath, "that was quite the greeting."

"We all have our forms of saying hello. You assault people on sidewalks, and I—" He cupped her chin again, kissing her deeply.

When their lips finally parted, she murmured, "I hope you don't greet all the girls like that."

"Just one. And only one, from here on out."

Her eyes widened, searching his expression.

"I know you said you can't leave Fern and Hope Hideaway, but we'll make it work. I love you, Kat Bennet. And I can't go back to the way things were before you walked into my life. And neither can this guy. He's been moping around like a lovesick puppy ever since you left."

Kneeling to nuzzle Fitz's neck, she told him, "I love you, too, buddy," her voice thick with emotion.

Jack's heart sputtered, aching to hear those same words.

As she stood, she met his gaze. "I love you, too, Jack."

Her breathy whisper set every nerve in his body on edge, and his throat went dry. Once again, all thoughts escaped him except for one.

Gathering Kat in his arms, he lowered his mouth to hers, savoring every spine-tingling sensation as he lost himself in a moment of pure, unparalleled joy.

Fitz waited patiently, leaning against Jack's leg until he grew restless and released a whimpering sigh.

Kat laughed softly. "I think someone needs attention."

"Like I said, we've got ourselves quite the little beggar."

"We?"

"Yep. You'd better get used to hearing me say that. *We* have a dog. And *we* have an inn…."

He let that last sentence linger in the air between them, gauging her reaction. Since she'd known where to find him, he assumed someone—most likely Penny—had mentioned something about it.

"We have an inn?" she repeated slowly, clearly stunned.

"Penny didn't tell you?"

"She told me where to find you, but didn't say what you were doing out here."

"In that case…" With an arm around her waist, Jack swiveled so they both faced the sprawling home. "What do you think of our new inn?"

"I—I don't know what to say," she stammered, still in shock. "Is it really ours?"

"It sure is. We can work out the logistics with you in Starcross Cove, but I want it to run exactly as you'd imagined it."

"It's incredible, Jack." She ran a finger along the corner of her eye, brushing aside a stray tear. "And the logistics won't be a problem."

"What do you mean?" He felt his heartbeat skip, hardly daring to hope.

"I'm moving to Poppy Creek."

He earnestly searched her face, praying he hadn't dreamt her words. "Are you really staying?"

She gazed up at him, her cheeks flushed and radiant.

In a single glance, it was as if he could see their entire future.

And it had never looked brighter.

CHAPTER 31

*a*s Kat gazed in the floor-length mirror, she hardly recognized herself. So much had changed in such a short amount of time.

The last several days had flown by in a whirlwind of wedding planning and settling into Penny's apartment. Since Trudy had booked her room with new guests after she'd left, every night at Penny's had become an old-fashioned slumber party. They'd baked cookies in their pajamas, watched classic Christmas movies, and stayed up way too late giggling about boys.

Well, two boys in particular.

In all her life, Kat had never felt more wholly content. And it showed in the glow of her skin and the bright glimmer in her eyes.

"You look stunning." Penny stood beside her, joining her reflection in the mirror.

The vintage gold gown cascaded over Kat's curves, grazing the tops of her satin, peep-toe heels. Her red curls had been swept to the side, pinned in place with a pearl-studded comb, revealing her bare neck.

"So do you," Kat murmured, admiring her sister's graceful

silhouette. The shimmering silver dress fit her like a dream, and she'd never looked more beautiful. She'd also never looked more like their mother. But this time, the similarities made Kat's heart ache a little less. Her guilt and bitterness had vanished, replaced by a sense of peace and hope for the future. "The dress looks like it was made for you."

"It does, doesn't it?" Penny swayed her hips, smiling as the feathers danced with the subtle movement.

"Everything is exactly as it should be." Kat sniffled, suddenly overcome with emotion as memories of the day's events came flooding back.

They'd spent Christmas morning with Colt and his family at Luke and Cassie's home, celebrating with familiar faces and a few new ones. Kat met Cassie's mother, Donna, along with Eliza's parents, Hank and Sylvia. Frank and Beverly were there, too, glowing like dreamy-eyed newlyweds. And Fitz had a grand time rollicking in the snow with Grant and Eliza's son, Ben, and their dog, Vinny.

After breakfast—during which Kat had made Fern's hot chocolate and Jack served his scrumptious flapjacks—they called Fern to wish her a merry Christmas. She'd raved about the coffee and sweets Kat had sent for everyone at Hope Hideaway. And for Fern, she'd included a special edition of *A Christmas Carol*, complete with the most exquisite illustrations.

To Fern's delight, Kat and Jack promised to visit the following weekend, and Kat couldn't wait for the two of them to meet in person. Although Jack never revealed that he'd been the one to save the shelter, Kat knew the truth in her heart. And she loved him all the more for his quiet, selfless act of generosity.

They'd also made plans for Fern to visit Poppy Creek in the new year, and the mere thought of her two worlds melding together had stirred tears of joy.

Penny squeezed her hand, her own eyes glistening. "It really has been magical, hasn't it?"

"And surreal. My whole life has changed. And to think, it all started with the search for Helena's brooch."

Releasing her grasp, Penny reached beneath her veil on the dressing table. With a wistful smile, she asked, "You mean this brooch?"

Kat sucked in a breath as the late afternoon sunlight filtered through the gossamer curtains, causing the imitation gems to sparkle. She'd almost forgotten how beautiful it was. "It's so lovely, it's hard to believe it isn't real."

"It's real," Penny said with a slight catch in her voice. "Just not in the way we expected." She stepped forward, unclipping the pin on the back. "And I think Helena would be glad you found it."

"*We* found it," Kat corrected, her throat tightening.

"Without you, I wouldn't have even known it was missing." Misty-eyed, Penny secured the sprig of mistletoe to the front of Kat's dress. "It belongs with you."

Too overwhelmed to speak, Kat caressed the smooth stones, blinking back tears.

"You know, I used to wish Helena had never left us," Penny admitted in a shaky whisper. "But then, I wouldn't have you." She traced a fingertip beneath her lashes, careful not to smudge her mascara. "It's one of life's many mysteries, isn't it? How God can take something broken and make it beautiful."

"You know what they call that?" Kat asked with a soft smile.

"What?"

"A miracle."

✳

*J*ack hopped out of his truck and straightened his plaid tie.

Normally, he didn't believe weddings should be held on holidays because they interfered with family time. But in this case, Penny and Colt *were* his family. And as he strode toward the chapel at the top of the hill, he didn't think they could have chosen a more perfect day or venue.

The tall steeple covered in snow glittered in the sunlight like a beacon announcing the celebration. And the fragrant evergreen wreath with a red satin bow popped against the backdrop of white. Simple and tasteful, just like he imagined his and Kat's wedding would be one day.

The thought made him grin.

"You look pretty happy for a man without a date."

Startled, Jack nearly slipped on a patch of ice.

Lucy stood by the front steps wearing a smirk.

"Luce? What are you doing here?" Jack wobbled, regaining his footing.

"Merry Christmas to you, too," she laughed. "Kat invited me. She said you needed a plus-one since she's in the bridal party."

Jack smiled. Of course Kat had invited her, knowing how special it would be to have his sister visit on Christmas. He already knew she was the kindest, most loving woman alive, yet she continued to amaze him with her generous heart.

Refocusing on Lucy, he asked, "What about Mom's shindig?"

She shrugged. "We've already done all the planning. She doesn't need me there. Besides, I told her this was more important."

He swallowed, too stunned to speak.

"You're not going to turn me down, are you? I bought a new dress for the occasion." She swished the hem of her burgundy gown, which was partially hidden by her wool cloak.

"Any excuse to go shopping, huh?" he teased, lightening the mood before his emotions turned him into a blubbering mess.

Offering his arm, he escorted his sister up the stone steps.

"You should have seen your face," Lucy giggled. "For a second, I thought you might fall and break your neck."

"So did I," he chuckled.

"Well, you might want to grab the railing, because I have another surprise."

"Oh, yeah?"

"Kat told me about the inn."

Jack paused at the top of the stairs. "She did?"

"Yep. And that's not all." Lucy's grin widened. "She offered me a job."

"A job?" Apparently, the shock had reduced his vocabulary to one-syllable words.

"She said the inn probably won't be ready until the fall, but when it is, she'd like me to decorate it."

Whenever Jack didn't think he could possibly love Kat more, she proved him wrong. "What did you say?"

"I already told Dad to look for my replacement."

"Seriously?"

"Staging houses is fun and all, but decorating a historic inn would be an exciting challenge. Kat says she wants it to have modern comfort while also remaining true to the original architecture with period-appropriate whimsy and charm. Honestly, the job is a dream come true."

As Jack listened to his sister, a lump formed in his throat.

She may not realize it, but her dream wasn't the only one coming true.

*A*fter the ceremony, the town square buzzed with merriment as wedding guests mingled with carnival goers. Lighthearted games and lively music paired with the tantalizing aroma of candied chestnuts and spiced apple cider to create a magical winter wonderland.

Basking in their newlywed glow, Penny and Colt disappeared in the crowd of well-wishers, and Lucy scampered off to greet old friends. For a moment, Kat felt as if she and Jack were the only two people in the world.

Her heart full, she leaned against him, enjoying the weight of his arm wrapped around her shoulders.

"I have to hand it to Mayor Burns," Jack said with a bemused chuckle. "The Christmas Carnival wasn't the worst idea, after all."

Kat smiled in agreement. "The storefront displays look wonderful."

As they strolled the town square, they admired the abundance of creativity, pointing out their favorite features.

The hardware store had built a sleigh using an assortment of tools and household fixtures, and Mac's Mercantile constructed a life-size Santa Claus out of produce and food staples, right down to the cauliflower beard and a belly made from a literal bowl full of jelly.

When they paused in front of Jack's Diner, Kat's heart warmed as her gaze rested on their arbor covered in frosted mistletoe. They'd also added ribbons and baubles, along with crystal icicles, and in Kat's opinion, the entrance to the diner rivaled the gateway to the North Pole.

"Are you ready for the big reveal?" Jack glanced at the clock tower on the courthouse. "I set the timer so the lights would go on at exactly six o'clock."

When the big hand hit the twelve, the arbor illuminated in a flash of glittering light.

Kat gasped as the gold and silver bulbs twinkled amid the lush greenery. "Jack, it's beautiful."

Even though she'd designed a similar display in Starcross Cove, the splendor of what she'd created with Jack far surpassed her expectations.

"Care for a closer look?" Taking her hand, he led her beneath the archway.

Enveloped in festive sprigs studded with tiny, shimmering stars, Kat gaped in breathless awe.

"Do you know why people kiss under mistletoe?" Jack stood so close, she felt his warmth clear through her coat and scarf.

Trying to focus on his question—and not the overwhelming urge to kiss him right then and there—she murmured, "I have no idea."

"The truth is, no one knows for sure. But there's one legend I'm particularly fond of." He smiled and the sight made her heart flutter just like the first time they met.

"In Norse mythology, the nefarious god Loki used a spear made out of mistletoe to kill the son of Frigg, the goddess of love. When the gods were able to bring her son back to life, Frigg declared the mistletoe a symbol of love, and promised to kiss anyone who passed beneath it. I like this version of the legend because it's all about redemption."

"It is?" Kat asked, not following his logic.

"For the mistletoe. You see, it could've gone down in history as the plant that killed Frigg's son. Instead, it became a symbol of love. And if couples don't kiss when they're underneath it, they'll have bad luck." He met her gaze, his lips quirked in a mischievous grin.

"Bad luck?"

"Atrocious, awful, appalling luck." He inched closer, and a tingle skittered down her spine.

"Well, we certainly don't want that, do we?"

As Jack lowered his lips to hers, playfully sealing their good fortune, a whisper of hope washed over her.

No matter what life brought their way, they would look for the good.

And together, she knew they would find it.

EPILOGUE

$\mathcal{A}$s Reed Hollis cradled the cup of hot chocolate warming his hands, he observed the Christmas Carnival festivities unfolding in front of him as though he were watching a movie.

He couldn't help feeling a sense of detachment, noticing how everyone else's lives seemed to move on without him. In the past year alone, all of his closest friends had either gotten married or engaged. And as they huddled around the fire pit together—two-by-two except for Reed—the contrast had never been more pronounced.

But Reed had resigned himself long ago to being perpetually single.

How could he settle down when his heart remained firmly in the past?

"Do you think they'll give anyone else a chance under the mistletoe?" Grant chuckled, gazing at Jack and Kat canoodling under the arbor.

"I think it's sweet." Cassie snuggled closer to Luke, tucked into the crook of his arm.

"It's kind of a strange tradition, when you think about it," Colt pointed out. "Isn't mistletoe poisonous?"

"It's also a parasite," Luke added. "Some of the lumber I work with comes from trees that were killed by mistletoe."

Reed bristled on behalf of the misunderstood plant. It often got a bad rap, but as a horticulturist, he'd learned even weeds had their use. Plants—among many things in life—were rarely all good or all evil. And he often came to their defense. "While it's poisonous to humans, many animals rely on it for sustenance," he explained. "And early research shows an extract from the plant might be beneficial in fighting cancer."

"Really?" Penny asked, sounding particularly intrigued by the information. "Mistletoe is quite multifaceted, isn't it? It can mean so many different things to different people."

"Yep." He smiled behind the rim of his paper cup, appreciating her observation. She'd articulated one of the qualities he loved most about plants in general, especially flowers. Each one had been given a meaning. A white rose stood for innocence and purity, while a blue one, the rarest of them all, represented something wholly unique and unparalleled. And yet, each bud could also hold special meaning for specific individuals—whether it was simply someone's favorite flower or marked an important occasion.

"Well, ten bucks says they're next." Colt nodded toward Jack and Kat, who still appeared lost in their own mistletoe-covered world.

"I'll take that bet," Penny told him. "Eliza and Grant already have their date set for the spring."

"That didn't stop you two from beating us to the altar," Eliza laughed good-naturedly.

"That's true." Penny blushed.

"And it still didn't come quick enough." Colt swooped in for a kiss.

"Hey! Save it for the honeymoon," Luke chided with a playful nudge.

"Where are you two going?" Reed asked, realizing they'd never mentioned it.

"Back to Greece," Penny answered quickly, beaming in delight.

"Only this time, without my mom as a chaperone." Colt grinned.

"Sounds heavenly," Cassie said with a dreamy sigh. "Although, I'd go back to Paris in a heartbeat."

"Me too," Luke agreed with an affectionate smile, drawing his wife closer to his side.

As they chatted about all the places they'd traveled, Reed remained silent.

He'd only ever ventured outside of California once, on an ill-fated trip to New York City he'd rather forget. He shuddered, suppressing the unpleasant memory.

"How are the wedding plans coming along?" Penny asked Eliza.

"Slower than I'd like. There are so many little details to coordinate. I've always wanted a big, elaborate wedding. But I underestimated the amount of work."

"If only we knew an event planner who could help," Grant teased.

"Your sister lives all the way on the East Coast," Eliza reminded him. "Not to mention, she has the busiest, most glamorous lifestyle I've ever seen. I doubt she'd have time in between all of her celebrity clients. Just taking time off to come home for the wedding is a huge favor."

Reed shuffled his feet, fighting the urge to extricate himself from the conversation.

He'd tried not to think about the fact that Olivia would be returning to Poppy Creek in a few months for Grant's wedding.

Because the only thing worse than running into the woman who'd broken your heart was seeing her on the arm of another man.

Especially a guy like Steven Rockford III.

While Reed lived in worn Levi's with perpetual dirt stains and drove a renovated VW van, Steven wore Armani suits and had a hired car service. The two men didn't simply reside on opposite ends of the country, they inhabited two completely different worlds.

"I'm sure she's not *that* busy," Grant assured her. "I bet she'd be happy to help. Want me to ask?"

No sooner than the question had left his lips, Grant's mother, Harriet, pushed through the crowd, her usually composed features strained and ashen.

"What's wrong?" Grant's demeanor shifted the instant he spotted his mother's worried expression.

"Have you heard from your sister?"

"No. I left a voice mail yesterday, but haven't heard back yet."

"That's what concerns me. I've been calling nonstop the last few days. I figured she and Steven were busy with holiday plans. But she's never *not* called to wish us a merry Christmas. I think something might be wrong."

A cold dread settled over Reed as he listened to the exchange.

If anything had happened to Olivia, he didn't know what he'd do.

Losing the woman he loved to another man had been unbearable.

But at least she'd seemed happy. He couldn't stand the thought of anything less.

Stepping away from the circle, he slipped out his phone, preparing to do the one thing he'd vowed against.

Contact Olivia Parker.

You can continue Reed's story and find out what happened to Olivia in *The Faith in Flowers.*

But before you go, **I have a special gift for you**. Visit rachaelbloome.com/secret-garden-club to download a bonus scene featuring Colt and Penny's wedding.

*I*f you enjoyed Jack and Kat's story, please consider leaving a short review. Even a few words can help a potential reader discover the beloved world of Poppy Creek.

ACKNOWLEDGMENTS

As I prepared to publish my second Christmas novel, and the fourth book in my Poppy Creek series, I was overcome with gratitude for how many people have come alongside me on my author journey. I wouldn't be where I am today without each and every one of them.

First, I'd like to thank my incredible ARC Team—You've all been so generous with your time and instrumental in ensuring that each launch is as successful as possible. My deepest, heartfelt thanks goes to:

Alethea Bjune, Amy Baker, Annalisa Turner, Annette Sullivan, Bernadette Cinkoske, Carol Schmoker, Cynthia Alexander, Dawn Najpaver, Diane Laverick, Diane Moreci, Elsie Nicolette, Emily Dill, Gwenn Henderson Eyer, Heather Womboldt, Ingrid Vitalis, Jean Cottrell, Judy Frayne, Kim Pierce, Kirby B, Kristy Fluckiger, Lesley Eyre, Lisa Roth, Lisa Wetzel, Lori Raines, Michelle Severt, Muriel Logan, Pam Merrill, Pamela Bandy-Dafoe, Patti Moore Clack, Paula Cox Hurdle, Peggy Potempa, Penny Leidecker, Rebecca Brewster, Rhonda Freeman, Robin

White, Sandra Tuozzo, Sherry Izell, Sherry Johanson, Vivian Morgan, and Wendy Gnau (a particularly talented typo catcher).

Next, I'd like to thank my brilliant design and editing team who turn my jumble of words into a finished product.

Ana—Your creativity never ceases to amaze me. And each new cover you design inevitably becomes my favorite.

Beth—I'm so thankful to have an editor I trust explicitly, who preserves my "voice" while transforming my prose into a polished, professional novel.

Krista—You continue to go above and beyond, proving to be the best proofreader in the biz as well as a dear friend.

Dave—You are my first line of defense. Or is it offense? I'm not sure. Either way, you see my chapters before anyone else. And your feedback and words of encouragement are often what inspire me to sit down and write the next page, which is a gift I can never repay.

Trenda—Your notes and insights were invaluable as I prepared to send this novel out into the world. Having a fresh pair of eyes read the story from start to finish gave me the confidence I needed to finally convince myself that it was ready.

Gigi, Mel, and Sarah—You ladies mean so much to me. I cherish our online chats and can't wait for the day we can finally have one in person.

Lynn, Cheryl, and Patti—Special thanks to you three for putting in the long hours to proof my audiobooks so I could focus on writing. You're a dream team, and I'm so grateful.

Pam and Adam of Vanguard Krav Maga—I miss you both dearly and look forward to a time when I can throw some more elbows with my Krav family.

For all the lovely men and women in my Facebook group— You've turned our little corner of the internet into a fun, welcoming space where I often go for advice. As someone who was previously social media shy, I can't thank you enough for being so kind and loving. I sincerely enjoy all of our online "get-togethers."

Unending love and appreciation for my incredible family—I wouldn't be where I am today without you.

And last, but not least—Many heartfelt thanks to you, dear reader, for returning to Poppy Creek with me for the fourth book in the series. I hope we have many more visits ahead of us.

All my love and gratitude,

ABOUT THE AUTHOR

Rachael Bloome is a *hopeful* romantic. She loves every moment leading up to the first kiss, as well as each second after saying, "I do." Torn between her small-town roots and her passion for traveling the world, she weaves both into her stories—and her life!

Joyfully living in her very own love story, she enjoys spending time with her husband and two rescue dogs, Finley and Monkey. When she's not writing, helping to run the family coffee roasting business, or getting together with friends, she's busy planning their next big adventure!

You can learn more about Rachael and her books at rachaelbloome.com

PEQUEÑOS MILAGROS RECIPE

FERN'S TINY MIRACLES

Ingredients

For Cookies:

* * *

1 1/2 cup softened butter

3/4 cup powdered sugar

3 tsp vanilla extract

3 cups all-purpose flour

1/4 tsp salt

1 cup chopped cinnamon-roasted pecans *recipe at the end (or regular roasted pecans)

* * *

For Cinnamon & Sugar Coating:

1/2 cup granulated sugar

1 Tbs ground cinnamon

* * *

Instructions:

Preheat oven to 350 degrees.

* * *

Combine butter, powdered sugar, and vanilla in a large mixing bowl. Beat at medium-high speed until completely blended.

In a separate bowl, combine flour and salt.

Gradually add the flour mixture to the butter mixture until completely combined.

Carefully fold in the pecans.

Roll dough into 1-inch balls, coat in cinnamon and sugar, and place approximately 2 inches apart on a nonstick (or lightly greased) cookie sheet.

Bake for 15 minutes.

Remove from oven and immediately roll in cinnamon and sugar a second time.

* * *

Enjoy!

* * *

Alternate Powdered Sugar Coating:

Ingredients:

3/4 cup powdered sugar

1/4 tsp salt

Instructions:

Combine powdered sugar and salt in a medium size bowl.

Once you've removed the cookies from the oven, immediately roll in powdered sugar mixture and place on a rack to cool.

Once cooled, coat in powdered sugar a second time.

Optional:

Add a dash of freshly ground star anise to cinnamon and sugar mixture, to taste.

* * *

Cinnamon Roasted Pecans:

Ingredients

2 1/4 cup pecan halves

2 Tbs egg whites (or 1 large egg white)

1 Tbs water

1/2 cup granulated sugar

1/4 tsp salt

1 1/2 tsp ground cinnamon

* * *

Instructions:

Combine the egg white and water until fluffy.

Coat pecans evenly.

Combine sugar, salt, and cinnamon until well-blended.

Coat pecans evenly.

Spread pecans in a nonstick (or lightly greased) baking pan and bake until toasted and fragrant (about 1 hour) stirring every 20 minutes.

Allow to cool before chopping.

BOOK CLUB QUESTIONS

1. How did you feel about Kat's reaction to learning she had a half-sister? If you were in her shoes, would you have contacted your sister right away, waited a certain period of time or never reached out at all?

2. What did you think about Kat and Penny's reactions to meeting each other for the first time? Did the growth of their relationship feel authentic? How do you think you would react in a similar situation?

3. In her pain, Kat avoided talking about her mother and didn't tell Penny that Helena had passed away. How would you have handled things differently?

4. How do you think Jack should have handled the conflict with his father?

5. Fern told Kat that love is generous... what does this phrase mean to you?

6. What are your thoughts on Helena Bennet? Would you classify her as a villain, misunderstood or somewhere in between?

7. What are some of the themes you noticed in the novel?

As always, I'd love to hear your responses or answer any questions you might have. You can reach me at hello@rachaelbloome.com.

Made in the USA
Coppell, TX
14 December 2022

89177432R00132